Ingrid Matson Wekerle

The Little Big Book of
NEW YORK

The Little Big Book of
New York

LITERARY EXCERPTS, ESSAYS, RECIPES,
POETRY, SONGS, HISTORY, AND FACTS

Edited by Natasha Tabori Fried and Lena Tabori

welcome
BOOKS

New York • San Francisco

Published in 2004 by Welcome Books ®
An imprint of Welcome Enterprises, Inc.
6 West 18th Street, New York, NY 10011
(212) 989-3200; Fax (212) 989-3205
www.welcomebooks.biz

Publisher: Lena Tabori
Project Director: Natasha Tabori Fried
Designer: Jon Glick
Facts, Histories, and Recipe Introductions: Zoë Schneider
Additional Facts: Peter Lubell
Recipes: Sasha Perlraver
Editorial assistants: Lawrence Chesler, Bethany Cassin
Beckerlegge, Nicholas Mancini

Distributed to the trade in the U.S. and Canada by
Andrews McMeel Distribution Services
Order Department and Customer Service
Toll-free: (800) 943-9839
Orders-only Fax: (800) 943-9831

Library of Congress Cataloging-in-Publication Data

The little big book of New York / edited by Natasha Tabori
Fried, Lena Tabori.
      p. cm. – (16th in the Little big book series)
      ISBN: 0-932183-02-7
      1. New York (N.Y.)—Literary collections. 2. New York
(N.Y.) —Miscellanea. 3. New York (N.Y.)—Anecdotes. I. Fried,
Natasha. II. Tabori, Lena. III Little big book (New York, N.Y.) ; 16th.

PS549.N5L58 2004
810.8'0327471—dc22

                                                    2003064733

Printed in Singapore
First Edition
10 9 8 7 6 5 4 3 2 1

CONTENTS

SONGS

POETRY

RECIPES

FACT SPREADS

A hundred times have I thought New York is a catastrophe, and fifty times: It is a beautiful catastrophe.

—LE CORBUSIER

THE HISTORY OF *DAUPHINE* AND ITS VOYAGES

GIOVANNI DA VERRAZANO

AT THE END OF A HUNDRED LEAGUES, we found a very pleasant site placed among some rising hills, in the midst of which there ran towards the sea a very large river, which was deep at its mouth, and from the sea to the hills there, on the flood tide, which we found eight feet, there might have passed ships of any burthen....We proceeded with a boat to enter the river and land, which we found very populous, and the people much like the others, dressed with birds' feathers of diverse colors. They came towards us joyfully, emitting very great shouts of admiration, showing us where, with the boat, it was safest to land....In a moment, as often happens in navigating, a violent contrary wind from the sea blowing up, we were forced to return to the ship, leaving the said land with much regret, considering that from its convenience and pleasant aspect it could not but have some valuable quality....

BETWEEN 1892 AND 1924, 16 million immigrants entered America through Ellis Island—71 percent of all immigrants in the United States—seeking freedom of speech, freedom of religion, and economic opportunities.

Located in upper New York Bay, Ellis Island was originally known to Native Americans as "Kioshk," or Gull Island, for its resident birds. Samuel Ellis acquired it in 1785, and in 1808 the state of New York purchased it from his descendants, turning it over to the federal government for $10,000. It was barely used until 1890, when President Benjamin Harrison designated Ellis Island as a federal immigration station.

Fifteen-year-old Annie Moore from County Cork, Ireland, was the first of 700 immigrants to be processed on January 1, 1892—Ellis Island's opening day. Approximately 450,000 more immigrants were admitted that first year. In 1897, fire destroyed the original buildings along with all records. A fireproof replacement designed to accommodate up to half a million immigrants a year opened on December 17, 1900, but was soon unable to handle the increasing number of immigrants. The government enlarged the island with landfill from the Grand Central Station excavation, increasing Ellis Island from its original three acres to 27.5 acres, and constructed 33 additional buildings.

The center of activity was the Registry Room (or Great Hall), where Public Health Service and the Bureau of Immigration (later known as the Immigration and Naturalization Service, or the INS) welcomed immigrants or denied them entry. Those not allowed included criminals, polygamists, paupers, contract laborers, and people suffering from debilitating or contagious illnesses. Back then, more than 98 percent of prospective immigrants gained entry—80 percent in eight hours or less.

In 1907, Ellis Island experienced its highest number of immigrants in a single year: about 1.25 million. With the onset of World War I and decreased immigration to the U.S., the island was used as an Army hospital and detention center for suspected enemy aliens. During this time, immigrants were inspected onboard ships or at the docks and a literacy test was introduced, which remained a standard until 1952. Those over 16 who could not read 30–40 test words in their own language were not admitted. Asian immigrants were almost entirely banned. In 1920, the island reopened as an immigration receiving station, processing 225,206 people.

After World War I, America opened embassies worldwide and immigrants applied for visas at consulates in their own countries. After 1924, the only people detained at Ellis Island were those with paperwork problems, war refugees, or deportees. During World War II, enemy merchant seamen were detained on the island while the Coast Guard trained about 60,000 servicemen there. The island was finally officially closed in November of 1954 when the INS moved its office to Manhattan.

President Lyndon Johnson declared Ellis Island part of the Statue of Liberty National Monument in 1965. In 1982, Ronald Reagan formed a commission to set up a private foundation to collect donations for the restoration of Ellis Island and the Statue of Liberty. It was the largest historic restoration in U.S. history, beginning in 1984 with a budget of $160 million dollars. The Main Building was restored to look as it did between 1918 and 1924, and reopened on September 10, 1990 as the Ellis Island Immigration Museum. Today, it receives almost two million visitors each year.

MANNAHATTA

WALT WHITMAN

I was asking for something specific and perfect for
    my city
Whereupon lo! upsprang the aboriginal name.
New I see what there is in a name, a word, liquid,
    sane,
        unruly, musical, self-sufficient,
I see that the word of my city is that word from of old,
Because I see that word nested in nests of water-bays,
    superb,
Rich, hemm'd thick all around with sailships and
        steamships, an island sixteen miles long,
        solid-founded,
Numberless crowded streets, high growths of iron,
        slender, strong, light, splendidly uprising toward
        clear skies,
Tides swift and ample, well-loved by me, toward
        sundown,
The flowing sea-currents, the little islands, larger
        adjoining islands, the heights, the villas,
The countless masts, the white shore-steamers, the
        lighters, the ferry-boats, the black sea-steamers
        well-model'd,

The down-town streets, the jobbers' houses of
    business, the houses of business of the ship-
    merchants and money-brokers, the river-streets,
Immigrants arriving, fifteen or twenty thousand in
    a week,
The carts hauling goods, the manly race of drivers of
    horses, the brown-faced sailors,
The summer air, the bright sun shining, and the sailing
    clouds aloft,
The winter snows, the sleigh-bells, the broken ice in
    the river, passing along up or down with the
    flood-tide or ebb-tide,
The mechanics of the city, the masters, well-form'd,
    beautiful-faced, looking you straight in the eyes,
Trottoirs throng'd, vehicles, Broadway, the women,
    the shops and shows,
A million people—manners free and superb—open
    voices—hospitality—the most courageous and
    friendly young men,
City of hurried and sparkling waters! city of spires
    and masts!
City nested in bays! my city!

HUDSON RIVER

In April of 1609, Captain Henry Hudson, renowned explorer of Arctic waters, set out from Amsterdam in search of an all-water route to Asia. He began his exploration of the river now named for him on September 12 of that year.

The first coherent school of American art was called the Hudson River School. Developed by such landscape painters as Thomas Cole and Asher Durand in the mid-19th century, the style took a Romantic approach to depicting the Hudson River and the Catskill, Berkshire, and White Mountains, as well as other sites further west.

Steamboat inventor Robert Fulton's successful navigation of the Hudson in a steamboat from New York City to Albany in 1807 revolutionized commercial enterprise in the state and enabled New York City to become the financial cultural epicenter it is today.

Actor Roy Harold Scherer, Jr, was given his stage name by his agent, who combined the "Rock of Gibraltar" with the name of the Hudson River. The actor became Rock Hudson, of course.

Washington Irving's works "The Legend of Sleepy Hollow" and "Rip Van Winkle"

both grew out of folklore of
the Hudson River region.

※

The Hudson River travels through
315 miles of mountains, farmlands,
and towns, flowing by the port cities
of Albany, Newburgh, Kingston,
Poughkeepsie, and Yonkers,
passing the Palisades, and finally
arriving at New York City.

※

The Hudson River Maritime
Museum hosts the annual Kingston
Shad Festival on the first weekend
in May to celebrate the return of the
shad to the Hudson River. Unusual
among freshwater fish, shad are
anadromous, meaning they spend
the bulk of their lives in the
ocean and only return to fresh
water to reproduce.

THE RIVERMEN

JOSEPH MITCHELL

I often feel drawn to the Hudson River, and I have spent a lot of time through the years poking around the part of it that flows past the city. I never get tired of looking at it; it hypnotizes me. I like to look at it in midsummer, when it is warm and dirty and drowsy, and I like to look at it in January, when it is carrying ice. I like to look at it when it is stirred up, when a northeast wind is blowing and a strong tide is running—a new-moon tide or a full-moon tide—and I like to look at it when it is slack. It is exciting to me on weekdays, when it is crowded with ocean craft, harbor craft, and river craft, but it is the river itself that draws me, and not the shipping, and I guess I like it best on Sundays, when there are lulls that sometimes last as long

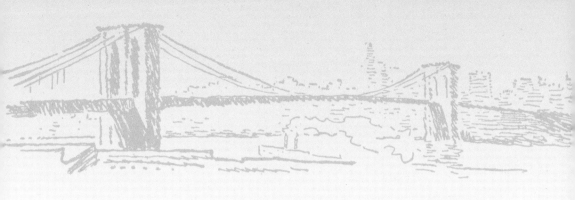

as half an hour, during which, all the way from the Battery
to the George Washington Bridge, nothing moves upon it,
not even a ferry, not even a tug, and it becomes as hushed
an dark and secret and remote and unreal as a river in a
dream. Once, in the course of such a lull, on a Sunday
morning in April, 1950, I saw a sea sturgeon rise out of
the water. I was on the New Jersey side of the river that
morning, sitting in the sun on an Erie Railroad coal dock.
I knew that every spring a few sturgeon still come in from
the sea and go up the river to spawn, as hundreds of
thousands of them once did, and I had heard tugboatmen
talk about them, but this was the first one I had ever seen.
It was six or seven feet long, a big, full-grown sturgeon,
It rose twice, and cleared the water both times, and I
plainly saw its bristly snout and its shiny little eyes and its
white belly and its glistening, greenish-yellow, bony-plated,
crocodilian back and sides, and it was a spooky sight.

NEW YORK STATE OF MIND

BILLY JOEL

Some folks like to get away,
take a holiday from the neighborhood
hop a flight to Miami Beach or to
    Hollywood
But I'm takin' a Greyhound on the
    Hudson River line
I'm in a New York state of mind

I've seen all the movie stars,
in their fancy cars and their limousines
been high in the Rockies under the
    evergreens.
But I know what I'm needin'
and I don't want to waste more time,
I'm in a New York state of mind

It was so easy livin' day by day,
out of touch with the rhythm and
    blues
And now I need a little give and take
the *New York Times*
the *Daily News*

Comes down to reality
and it's fine with me cause I've let it
    slide
don't care if it's Chinatown or on
    Riverside
I don't have any reasons I've left them
    all behind,
I'm in a New York state of mind

GENERAL FACTS

The New York Post is the nation's oldest newspaper.

The New York Philharmonic is America's oldest orchestra.

The Cloisters, a branch of the Metropolitan Museum of Art, is the only museum in America dedicated exclusively to medieval art.

Very superstitious: The 13 Lincoln Tunnel tollbooths are numbered 1-12 and 23.

New York's longest subway line is the C, at 32.4 miles.

By 1900, there were almost 1,000 people per acre living in some sections of the Lower East Side, and by 1910, Manhattan reached its peak population of 2.3 million, compared with 1.5 million now. In 1930, the subway carried almost twice the number of riders that it does now.

New York's state bird is the bluebird.

Its state flower is the rose.

New York's Finest? Police.
New York's Bravest? Firemen.
New York's Strongest? Sanitation workers.

Who are New York's Boldest?
New York's 10,000 correction officers, who oversee 14,000 to 19,000 inmates daily in city jails. The slogan appears on Department of Correction buses and some letterheads.

Broadway is the longest city street in the world. It stretches 150 miles from Bowling Green to Albany.

Six New Yorkers have been elected President of the United States: Martin Van Buren, Chester A. Arthur, Grover Cleveland, Millard Fillmore, Theodore Roosevelt, and Franklin D. Roosevelt.

The most common surname in New York is Rodriguez, with 22,712 entries. Rounding out the top five are Williams with 18,236 entries; Smith with 16,316; Brown with 15,485; and Rivera with 14,831.

New York City's total area in square miles: 301.

New York was originally named for England's Duke of York.

New York became a state on July 26, 1788

New York's motto is "Excelsior."

Central Park is 843 acres–a larger area than the principality of Monaco–and contains more than 500,000 trees and shrubs.

The Statue of Liberty's index finger is eight feet long.

The Verrazano-Narrows Bridge is so long–4,260 feet–that the towers are a few inches out of parallel to accommodate the curvature of the earth.

Nearly half a million people pass through Grand Central Terminal each day.

The five boroughs were annexed to form New York City in 1898.

There are 80 different languages spoken in New York City.

New York's nickname? The Empire State.

CHOP SUEY

NOODLES:

1 pound chow mein noodles

$1/4$ cup soy sauce

2 tablespoons brown sugar

2 tablespoons oil

2 tablespoons oyster sauce

MARINADE:

1 cup soy sauce

2 tablespoons oil

1 tablespoon cornstarch

2 to 3 tablespoons brown sugar

3 slices crushed ginger

4 cloves crushed garlic

2 tablespoons oyster sauce

1 tablespoon cooking sherry or red wine vinegar

*C*hop Suey is based on a Cantonese term for "odds and ends" or "mixed pieces" and is a dish that does not exist in China. There are numerous theories regarding the origins of Chop Suey. The most widely accepted is that the dish was created in New York City in 1896 when Chinese ambassador Li Hung Chang was sent by the Chinese Emperor to meet with President Grover Cleveland to strengthen U.S./China relations. When Chang threw a party, his personal cook prepared a bland meal, reminiscent of a Chinese-style dish, to satisfy both the American and Chinese palates.

1. Boil noodles in water according to package instructions. Cook until tender. Drain and place in a large bowl. Add soy sauce, brown sugar, oil, and oyster sauce. Toss well.

2. Spray a large cooking pan with non-stick spray. Spread the noodles evenly into the pan. Bake at 350° F for 30 minutes, or until dry and crispy, turning every 10 minutes. Set aside and keep warm.

CHOP SUEY

CHOP SUEY MEAT:
*2 chicken breasts,
sliced into
very thin strips*

*2 to 3 pork chops,
sliced into
very thin strips*

VEGETABLES:
1 head broccoli

3 large carrots

1 bunch celery

*$1/_2$ pound
fresh mushrooms*

*$1/_2$ pound
Chinese snow peas*

*1 can sliced water
chestnuts, drained*

*1 can bamboo
shoots, drained*

*1 bundle
green onions*

2 tablespoons oil

3. Combine marinade ingredients and marinate meat while preparing vegetables.

4. Clean, wash, and slice the vegetables.

5. Bring a large pot of water to boil. Parboil all the vegetables except the water chestnuts, bamboo shoots, and green onions, for 45–60 seconds. Drain and dunk into an ice bath or run under cold water to stop the cooking process. Drain again and set aside.

6. Add 1 tablespoon of oil to a hot stir-fry pan. Remove garlic pieces and ginger from the meat marinade and add to the pan. Cooking in batches, add the meat and cook very quickly. Set aside and reserve marinade.

7. Add 1 tablespoon more of oil to the hot pan. Stir-fry green onions, bamboo shoots, and mushrooms for half a minute. Add mixed vegetables and half of reserved marinade. Cook quickly and place over bed of noodles.

8. Heat remaining marinade in pan. Add meat and toss to coat. Pour over vegetables and serve.

Serves 4 to 6.

SINCE THE DUTCH ARRIVED in New York City in the early 1600s, millions of immigrants have come seeking new opportunities, creating one of the world's most culturally rich and diverse communities. Originally shaped by Germans, Irish, Italians, and Jews in the 19th and early 20th century, the city had its second wave of immigration after WWII, with immigrants from Latin America, the Caribbean, and Asia.

New York's first official immigration center at Castle Garden opened in 1865 and processed immigrants until 1890. Ellis Island served as the entry point for more than 16 million immigrants between 1892 and 1924.

By 1855, New York City was the largest city in the western hemisphere, with a population of roughly 623,000. Between 1880 and 1919, more than 23 million people immigrated to the US. Of those, 17 million entered through New York City. The two largest groups were Russian Jews and Italians. From 1870 on, Jews from Eastern Europe fled from poverty and pogroms and settled on the Lower East Side in squalid tenements. Italians arrived in the late 19th century. By 1930 there were more than one million Italians inhabiting New York City.

The first Germans arrived around 1710; by 1900 they made up 25 percent of the population. From the 1820s to the 1850s, famine, religious oppression, and poverty brought many Irish. By 1860, they were 25 percent of the city's population. In 1890, 24,000 blacks inhabited New York City; in 1940, there were 460,000, or 6 percent of the population.

Many Chinese arrived in the 1800s, but the Chinese Exclusion Act of 1882 barred Chinese immigrants from naturalization, marking the first time an ethnic group had been excluded from the United States. In 1943, Congress repealed all exclusion acts, and by 1980 80 percent of the immigrants in New York City were Asian.

Jacob A. Riis, a Danish immigrant who came to New York in 1870, became a huge catalyst for urban social reform. Working as a police reporter, he published *How the Other Half Lives*, documenting the horrors of tenement life. He greatly influenced the tenement housing reform movement, which improved sanitary conditions, created public parks and playgrounds, and recognized the need for more schools. Also, many immigrants worked in the garment industry and their struggle shaped the American labor movement. The Triangle Shirtwaist factory fire in 1911, which killed 146 young immigrant women due to despicable factory conditions, spawned a heightened awareness of labor issues.

By 1920, nearly 40 percent of the city's population was foreign born. In 1924 Congress passed the National Origins Act, restricting immigration based on place of origin. Between 1900 and 1930, Jamaica, Barbados, and other West Indian groups unaffected by this law (as British colonies, they were part of Britain's generous quota) sent over 150,000 West Indians to New York City. In 1920 they accounted for 25 percent of the black population of Harlem.

The Depression led to a decline in immigration, and Jews fleeing Nazism made up 25 percent of the immigrants in the 1930s. Puerto Ricans and Latin Americans dominated post-war immigration, and by 1965, the Immigration Act ended discrimination based on national origin, resulting in immigration from all over Asia, Africa, and the Middle East.

In 1970, immigrants accounted for only 18 percent of the population, but by the 1990s, immigrants made up about one third. With 121 languages spoken, and a multitude of foreign language newspapers, magazines, and television and radio stations, New York City has truly become a melting pot, creating a home for each ethnic group seeking to start a new life in this country.

*T*he intellectual life is why I'm a New Yorker. It's why I stay here. I spend my summers in Europe, and if they ask me if I'm an American, I say, "No, I'm a New Yorker." I don't know about everyone else, but for me that's a positive statement.

—ALEXANDER ALLAND, JR.

PIZZA

DOUGH
1 teaspoon active dry yeast

$2/3$ cup warm water

2 cups all-purpose flour

1 teaspoon salt

2 tablespoons olive oil

Oil for bowl

Cornmeal for the pizza stone

TOPPING
2 cups tomato sauce

1 lb. mozzarella, shredded

$1/2$ cup grated Romano cheese

1 tablespoon dried basil

1 tablespoon dried oregano

1 teaspoon dried red pepper flakes

Pizza was originally food for poor people of Naples. The earliest form of pizza was a bread baked beneath the stones of a fire, seasoned with a variety of toppings, and used instead of plates and utensils to sop up broth or gravies. It is said that the idea of using bread as a plate came from the Greek and Egyptian flat bread. It was eaten by the working classes because it was an inexpensive and convenient food. In 1905, Gennaro Lombardi, who moved from Naples to Little Italy in 1905, opened the nation's first licensed pizzeria, Lombardi's Coal Oven Pizzaria Napoletana, on Spring Street, using his grandfather's dough recipe. American soldiers stationed in Italy during World War II are said to have brought back the taste for pizza, which made pizza a mainstream popular food all over the U.S. New York City invented the pizza parlor-style pizza by serving slices instead of a whole pie, and allowing customers to watch bakers in the front of the store instead of hiding them in the back. The art of making pizza dough is a New York City attraction in itself. It wasn't until the 1960s that pizza bakers first began twirling and tossing the dough for an audience. New York City has more pizzerias than any other American city.

PIZZA

This recipe requires a pizza stone to obtain the crust that New York pizza is famous for. One can be purchased at a specialty food store. You may use a cookie sheet, but you may find the results a little disappointing.

1. Preheat oven to 475° F.

2. Sprinkle yeast over warm water and let stand 1 minute. Stir until yeast dissolves.

3. In a large bowl, combine the flour, salt, and olive oil. Stir in the water and yeast until a soft dough forms. Knead for 5 minutes, adding more flour if dough gets too sticky or wet.

4. Coat a bowl with olive oil and place the dough inside, covering with plastic wrap. Allow to rise 1 1/2 hours.

5. Flatten dough on a floured work surface and roll dough out to a 12" circle. If you get inspired, toss it in the air a few times, trying to catch the edges, this helps to stretch the dough and creates a nice elasticity. It's also easier than rolling.

6. Place on a pizza stone that has been dusted with cornmeal.

7. Spread sauce almost to the edge of dough and cover with mozzarella, grated Romano cheese, basil, oregano, and red pepper flakes. Bake your pizza on bottom shelf of the oven for 12–15 minutes or until crispy and cheese is bubbly.

Yields one pizza (serves 4 to 6)

GOODBYE TO ALL THAT

JOAN DIDION

IT IS EASY TO SEE the beginnings of things, and harder to see the ends. I can remember now, with a clarity that makes the nerves in the back of my neck constrict, when New York began for me, but I cannot lay my finger upon the moment it ended, can never cut through the ambiguities and second starts and broken resolves to the exact place on the page where the heroine is no longer as optimistic as she once was. When I first saw New York I was twenty, and it was summertime, and I got off a DC-7 at the old Idlewild temporary terminal in a new dress which had seemed very smart in Sacramento but seemed less smart already, even in the old Idlewild temporary terminal, and the warm air smelled of mildew and some instinct, programmed by all the movies I had ever seen and all the songs I had ever heard sung and all the stories I had ever read about New York, informed me that it would never be quite the same again. In fact it never was. Some time later there was a song on all the jukeboxes on the upper East Side that went "but where is the schoolgirl who used to be me," and if it was late

enough at night I used to wonder that. I know now that almost everyone wonders something like that, sooner or later and no matter what he or she is doing, but one of the mixed blessings of being twenty and twenty-one and even twenty-three is the conviction that nothing like this, all evidence to the contrary notwithstanding, has ever happened to anyone before.

Of course it might have been some other city, had circumstances been different and the time been different and had I been different, might have been Paris or Chicago or even San Francisco, but because I am talking about myself I am talking here about New

York. That first night I opened my window on the bus into town and watched for the skyline, but all I could see were the wastes of Queens and the big signs that said MIDTOWN TUNNEL THIS LANE and then a flood of summer rain (even that seemed remarkable and exotic, for I had come out of the West where there was no summer rain), and for the next three days I sat wrapped in blankets in a hotel room air-conditioned to 35° and tried to get over a bad cold and a high fever. It did not occur to me to call a doctor, because I knew none, and although it did occur to me to call the desk and ask that the air conditioner be turned off, I never called, because I did not know how much to tip whoever might come—was anyone ever so young? I am here to tell you that some-one was. All I could do during those three days was talk long-distance to the boy I already knew I would never marry in the spring. I would stay in New York, I told him, just six months, and I could see the Brooklyn Bridge from my window. As it turned out the bridge was the Triborough, and I stayed eight years.

ENGLISHMAN IN NEW YORK

STING

I don't drink coffee I take tea, my dear.
I like my toast done on one side.
And you can hear it in my accent when I talk,
I'm an Englishman in New York.

You see me walking down Fifth Avenue,
A walking cane here at my side.
I take it ev'rywhere I walk.
I'm an Englishman in New York.

I'm an alien. I'm a legal alien.
I'm an Englishman in New York.
Woh. I'm an alien. I'm a legal alien.
I'm an Englishman in New York.

If "manners maketh man" as someone said,
He's the hero of the day.
It takes a man to suffer ignorance and smile.
Be yourself no matter what they say.

I'm an alien. I'm a legal alien.
I'm an Englishman in New York.
Woh. I'm an alien. I'm a legal alien.
I'm an Englishman in New York.

Modesty, propriety can lead to notoriety,
But you could end up as the only one.
Gentleness, sobriety are rare in this society.
At night a candle's brighter than the sun.

Takes more than combat gear to make a man.
Takes more than a license for gun.
Confront your enemies, avoid them when
    you can.
A gentleman will walk but never run.

If "manners maketh man" as someone said,
He's the hero of the day.
It takes a man to suffer ignorance and smile.
Be yourself no matter what they say.

Be yourself no matter what they say.
Be yourself no matter what they say.
Be yourself no matter what they say.
Be yourself no matter what they say.

FAMOUS NEW YORKERS

Throughout its history, New York has continually embraced the artist, the maverick, and the entrepreneur who have heeded the city's siren call. Once there, many eagerly left the lives and even the identities they'd had behind. They became "New Yorkers." So numerous are the people who've adopted New York as their home, any list of famous New Yorkers which included "transplants" would fill several volumes. Here, in an attempt to narrow the focus, only a select few of those born in New York State are included. So, writer F. Scott Fitzgerald, born in St. Paul, MN, whose chronicles of the rich and dissipated came to define the New York City of the 1920s, is absent. Actor Mel Gibson, who seems about as Australian as a boomerang, is in. He was born in Peekskill, NY.

Kareem Abdul-Jabbar, basketball player, *NYC*

Woody Allen, writer, director, actor, comedian, *Brooklyn*

James Baldwin, writer, *NYC*

Lucille Ball, actress, *Jamestown*

Humphrey Bogart, actor, *NYC*

Lenny Bruce, comedian, *Mineola*

James Cagney, actor, *NYC*

Maria Callas, soprano, *NYC*

Benjamin N. Cardozo, jurist, *NYC*

Willis Haviland Carrier, inventor of the air conditioner, *Angola*

Sean "P. Diddy" Combs, rap music mogul, *NYC*

Tom Cruise actor, *Syracuse*

Sammy Davis, Jr., actor, singer, *NYC*

Agnes de Mille, choreographer, *NYC*

George Eastman, inventor of film, *Waterville*

Gertrude Belle Elion, lukemia researcher, *NYC*

Millard Fillmore, president, *Locke*

Henry Louis Gehrig, baseball player, *NYC*

George Gershwin, composer, *Brooklyn*

Mel Gibson, actor, *Peekskill*

Jackie Gleason, comedian, actor, *Brooklyn*

Learned Hand, jurist, *Albany*

Joseph Heller, writer, *Brooklyn*

Edward Hopper, painter, *Nyack*

Washington Irving, author, *NYC*

Henry James, author, *NYC*

John Jay, jurist, *NYC*

Billy Joel, singer, composer, *Hicksville*

Michael Jeffery Jordan,
basketball player, *Brooklyn*

Jerome Kern, composer, *NYC*

Fiorello La Guardia, NYC mayor, *NYC*

Vince Lombardi, football coach, *NYC*

Chico, Groucho, Harpo,
Zeppo Marx, comedians, *NYC*

Herman Melville, author, *NYC*

Ethel Merman, singer, actress, *Astoria*

Arthur Miller, playwright, *NYC*

Henry Miller, writer, *NYC*

Ogden Nash, poet, *Rye*

Rosie O'Donnell, comedian, *Commach*

Eugene O'Neill, playwright, *NYC*

George Pullman,
inventor of the sleeper car, *Brocton*

Red Jacket, Seneca chief,
near Conaga, Seneca County

Christopher Reeve, actor, *NYC*

John D. Rockefeller, industrialist, *Richford*

Norman Rockwell, painter, illustrator, *NYC*

Mickey Rooney, actor, *Brooklyn*

Anna Eleanor Roosevelt, humanitarian, *NYC*

Franklin D. Roosevelt, president, *Hyde Park*

Theodore Roosevelt, president, *NYC*

Jonas Salk, polio researcher, *NYC*

Margaret Sanger,
women's rights activist, *Corning*

Elizabeth Cady Stanton, women's rights
pioneer, *Johnstown*

Barbra Streisand, singer, actress, *NYC*

Louis Comfort Tiffany,
painter, craftsman, *NYC*

Martin Van Buren, president, *Kinderhook*

Mae West, actress, *Brooklyn*

Edith Wharton, author, *NYC*

Walt Whitman, poet, *West Hills*

You know, the more they knock
New York, the bigger it gets.

—WILL ROGERS

RECUERDO

Edna St. Vincent Millay

We were very tired, we were very merry—
We had gone back and forth all night on the ferry.
It was bare and bright, and smelled like a stable—
But we looked into a fire, we leaned across a table,
We lay on a hill-top underneath the moon;
And the whistles kept blowing, and dawn came
    soon.

We were very tired, we were very merry—
We had gone back and forth all night on the ferry;
And you ate an apple, and I ate a pear,
From a dozen of each we had bought somewhere;
And the sky went wan, and the wind came cold,
And the sun rose dripping, a bucketful of gold.

We were very tired, we were very merry,
We had gone back and forth all night on the ferry.
We hailed, "Good morrow, mother!" to a shawl-
    covered head,
And bought a morning paper, which neither of us read;
And she wept, "God bless you!" for the apples and
    pears,
And we gave her all our money but our subway fares.

HERE IS NEW YORK

E. B. WHITE

THERE ARE ROUGHLY THREE NEW YORKS. There is, first, the New York of the man or woman who was born here, who takes the city for granted and accepts its size and its turbulence as natural and inevitable. Second, there is the New York of the commuter—the city that is devoured by locusts each day and spat out each night. Third, there is the New York of the person who was born somewhere else and came to New York in quest of something. Of these three trembling cities the greatest is the last—the city of final destination, the city that is a goal. It is the third city that accounts for New York's high-strung disposition, its poetical deportment, its dedication to the arts, and its incomparable achievements. Commuters give the city its tidal restlessness; natives give it solidity and continuity; but the settlers give it passion. And whether it is a farmer arriving from Italy to set up a small grocery store in a slum, or a young girl arriving from a small town in Mississippi to escape the indignity of being observed by her neighbors, or a boy arriving from the Corn Belt with a manuscript in his suitcase and a pain in his heart, it makes no difference: each embraces New York with the intense excitement of first love, each absorbs New York with the fresh eyes of an adventurer, each generates heat and light to dwarf the Consolidated Edison Company.

*B*eing a New Yorker means never

having to say you're sorry. —LILY TOMLIN

MOMENTS IN HISTORY

"Uncle Sam" was a meatpacker from Troy, New York. During the War of 1812, Sam Wilson stamped "U.S. Beef" on his barrels of meat and soldiers interpreted that as Uncle Sam.

In July of 1848, Elizabeth Cady Stanton, Lucretia Mott, and Jane Hunt orchestrated the first Woman's Rights Convention in Seneca Falls, New York. Nearly 300 people attended the event, where Stanton made her famous speech, "The Declaration of Rights and Sentiments."

On September 18, 1851, *The New York Times* published its inaugural issue. Before adopting its present name, the paper was known as the *New York Daily Times*.

On November 4, 1902, publisher William Randolph Hearst arranged for fireworks at Madison Square to celebrate being elected to Congress. The show, however, was poorly planned and a mortar containing 10,000 shells tipped over and caught fire. The ensuing explosion killed 17 people, injured 100, and blew out doors and windows on the square.

On August 28, 1774, the first American-born saint, Mother Elizabeth Ann Seton, was born in Lower Manhattan.

The New York Mercantile Exchange began as the Butter and Cheese Exchange in the 1750s.

The Empire State Building was lit with blue lights in 1995 to kick off the addition of blue M&M's, red pulsing lights to mark the release of Pink Floyd's album *Pulse*, and yellow for the debut of Microsoft Windows 95. They stopped doing requests after that—too many were made.

In September 1892, union workers in New York City took an unpaid day off and marched around Union Square in the city's first Labor Day parade, to fight for an eight-hour workday.

The *Titanic* was scheduled to arrive at Chelsea Piers on April 16, 1912. Fate intervened, and the "unsinkable" ship struck an iceberg and sank on April 14, 1912. Of the 2,200 passengers aboard, 675 were rescued by the Cunard liner *Carpathia*, which arrived at Chelsea Piers eight days later.

The New York Mets' first season in 1962 was the second worst in major league history: 40 wins and 120 losses. By 1968, the Mets finished in only ninth place, but late in the 1969 season they became forever known as the "Miracle Mets" when they captured their first World Series title in five games, with a 5–3 win over the Baltimore Orioles.

On May 19, 1962, more than 20,000 guests gathered for a Democratic fundraiser on President John F. Kennedy's birthday at Madison Square Garden. The highlight of the evening was Marilyn Monroe's breathy rendition of "Happy Birthday." Monroe wore a dress she had been sewn into minutes before, and which later sold at auction for almost $1.3 million.

TAMMANY HALL WAS a well-oiled political machine that dominated New York City from the mayoral victory of Fernando Wood in 1854 until the election of Fiorello H. LaGuardia in 1934.

After the Revolutionary War, numerous patriotic societies formed to promote political and economic interests. The Society of St. Tammany was founded in 1788 as a response to New York City's most elite and exclusive clubs. Although ultimately controlled by wealthy men, Tammany attracted support among the working classes and the immigrant population, mainly from Irish-American craftsmen.

In the early nineteenth century, Tammany supported progressive politics and opposed anti-Catholic and nativist movements. Throughout the 1830s and 1840s, it expanded its political influence by earning the loyalty of the many newly arriving immigrants; it helped newcomers to find jobs, housing, and obtain citizenship so that they would vote for Tammany candidates. In 1830, the group established its headquarters in Tammany Hall, making the name of the association and the location synonymous. Tammany soon became notorious for its political machine—the elected public officials used their influential positions to perpetuate the power of their political party, often through questionable means.

By the 1850s, Tammany had become famous for taking bribes, giving city contracts to members, and stealing funds from the city treasury. In 1863, former firefighter and chairmaker William M. "Boss" Tweed was elected to lead the general committee of Tammany. During his political reign, he served as a lawyer, county supervisor, state senator, and commissioner of public works. He also became one of the most famous crooks in New York City history. He purchased a printing company, which became the city's official printer, as well as a stationers' outfit, which sold supplies to the city at heavily inflated prices, and he used his law practice to extort money disguised as legal fees for various services rendered. Tweed invested the millions he siphoned from his corrupt business practices into real estate. By the late 1860s he was one of the city's largest landowners. He was instrumental in passing a new charter for the city for a Board of Audit, which was run by "the Tweed Ring." The Board supervised all city and county expenditures. From 1869 to 1871, the city's debt tripled, but Tweed's pockets overflowed.

Tammany Hall's corruption was eventually exposed through a series of cartoons by Thomas Nast and a *New York Times* article that disclosed the Tweed Ring's frauds. The Tweed Ring inflated payments for contractors building the city's new courthouse and all involved parties reaped the benefits. The courthouse cost over $13 million, which was more than twice what the United States had paid for Alaska just four years earlier. Tweed was arrested in October 1871 and convicted on 204 criminal counts, fined $12,750, and sentenced to twelve years in prison. It is estimated the Tweed Ring illegally gained $30–200 million dollars, but Tweed died in jail penniless in 1878.

After Tweed, John Kelly took control of Tammany Hall, creating a much-needed system of management. Unpaid precinct captains were appointed to specific neighborhoods to make sure everyone worked, had shelter, stayed out of trouble with the law, and voted. Tammany continued supporting progressive labor laws, opposing Prohibition and censorship, and survived into the 1930s from the collections of money and kickbacks. The Depression, however, brought social and cultural change. Franklin Delano Roosevelt was elected president and New Deal restrictions on immigration made voters less dependent on Tammany for jobs and assistance. The election of Fiorello LaGuardia finally removed City Hall from Tammany's control.

Today, the Tammany name and the term "machine politics" are still synonymous with political corruption.

PASTRAMI SANDWICH

*P*astrami is a dry-cured, smoked beef, usually made from a cut of plate, brisket, or round. The fat is trimmed, and the meat's surface is rubbed with salt and a seasoning generally made up of garlic, black and red pepper, cinnamon, cloves, allspice, and coriander seeds. The technique was adopted by Jewish peddlers who cured Kosher meat in the same fashion. Pastrami sandwiches can be served hot or cold, with mustard on rye bread. The pastrami sandwich is a New York deli staple and should always be served with a pickle. Wash it down with a seltzer or a root beer!

Dijon mustard

2 slices good quality rye bread

1/4 pound thinly sliced pastrami

1. Spread mustard on bread. Top with pastrami.

2. Slice in half and serve with a dill pickle and coleslaw.

VARIATION:
Rueben sandwiches are traditionally made with corned beef, but they can also be prepared with pastrami, making a great sandwich.

RUEBEN

sauerkraut

2 slices
Swiss cheese

1/4 pound thinly
sliced pastrami

Thousand Island
dressing

2 slices good
quality rye bread

1 tablespoon
butter

1. Heat sauerkraut in microwave for 30 seconds.

2. Lay cheese, pastrami, sauerkraut, and dressing on bread.

3. Heat a skillet over medium–high heat. Melt butter in skillet. Add sandwich and grill until cheese has melted and bread is golden on both sides.

4. Slice in half and serve with extra dressing, a dill pickle, and coleslaw.

Serves one.

THE DUEL

O. HENRY

NEW YORK CITY IS INHABITED by 4,000,000 mysterious strangers; thus beating Bird Centre by three millions and half a dozen nine's. They came here in various ways and for many reasons—Hendrik Hudson, the art schools, green goods, the stork, the annual dressmakers' convention, the Pennsylvania Railroad, love of money, the stage, cheap excursion rates, brains, personal column ads., heavy walking shoes, ambition, freight trains—all these have had a hand in making up the population.

But every man Jack when he first sets foot on the stones of Manhattan has got to fight. He has got to fight at once until either he or his adversary wins. There is no resting between rounds, for there are no rounds. It is slugging from the first. It is a fight to a finish.

Your opponent is the City. You must do battle with it from the time the ferry-boat lands you on the island until either it is yours or it has conquered you. It is the same whether you have a million in your pocket or only the price of a week's lodging.

The battle is to decide whether you shall become a New Yorker or turn the rankest outlander and Philistine. You must be one or the other. You cannot remain neutral. You must be for or against—lover or enemy—bosom friends or outcast. And, oh, the city is a general in the ring. Not only by blows does it seek to subdue you. It woos you to its heart with the subtlety of a siren. It is a combination of Delilah, green Chartreuse, Beethoven, chloral and John L. in his best days.

In other cities you may wander and abide as a stranger man as long as you please. You may live in Chicago until your hair whitens, and be a citizen and still prate of beans if Boston mothered you, and without rebuke. You may become a civic pillar in any other town but Knickerbocker's, and all the time publicly sneering at its buildings, comparing them with the architecture of Colonel Telfair's residence in Jackson, Miss., whence you hail, and you will not be set upon. But in New York you must be either a New Yorker or an invader of a modern Troy, concealed in the wooden horse of your conceited provincialism.

GET UP

PHILIP LEVINE

Morning wakens on time
in sub-freezing New York City.
I don't want to get out,
thinks the nested sparrow,
I don't want to get out
of my bed, says my son,
but out in Hudson Street
the trucks are grinding and honking
at United Parcel, and the voices
of loud speakers command us all.
The woman downstairs turns
on the TV and the smoke
of her first sweet joint rises
toward the infinite stopping
for the duration in my nostrils.
The taxpayers of hell are voting
today on the value of garbage,
the rivers are unfreezing
so that pure white swans may ride
upstream toward the secret source
of sweet waters, all the trains
are on time for the fun of it.
It is February of the year 1979
and my 52nd winter is turning
toward spring, toward cold rain
which gives way to warm rain
and beaten down grass. If I
were serious I would say I
take my stand on the edge
of the future tense and offer
my life, but in fact I stand
before a smudged bathroom mirror,
toothbrush in hand, and smile
at the puffed face smiling
back out of habit. Get up,
honey, I say, it could be a lot worse,
it could be a lot worse,
it could be happening to you.

TAKE ME BACK TO MANHATTAN

Cole Porter

Take me back to Manhattan.
Take me back to New York.
I'm just longing to see once more
My little home on the hundredth floor.
Can you wonder I'm gloomy?
Can you smile when I frown?

I miss the East side,
The West side,
The North side and
the South side;

So take me back to Manhattan,
That dear, old dirty town.

SKYSCRAPERS

The term "skyscraper" comes from sailor slang, meaning the tallest mast of a ship.

The real-estate boom in the late 19th century combined with the use of a steel frame and the personnel elevator were all factors in the rapid rise of the skyscraper craze.

New York City has the most skyscrapers in the world with more than 130.

The Flatiron building, built in 1902, is one of New York City's first skyscrapers.

Standing 47 stories high, the Singer Tower was the highest building in the world when it was completed in 1908 and became New York's first "tallest building in the world."

The Building Zone Resolution was passed in New York in 1916 to regulate the height and plans for buildings. It was intended to aid the health of city folk by allowing more light and air into the canyons created by the skyscrapers.

Sixty thousand people work at Rockefeller Center and 175,000 visit it daily.

The Woolworth Building, known for its gothic architecture, opened in 1913 on Broadway between Park Place and Barclay

Street. It was considered the tallest skyscraper in the world until 1930.

The Chrysler Building held the honor of world's tallest for less than a year—until the Empire State Building was completed.

When the Empire State Building was first opened, a plan was advocated for airships to use it for docking.

The Empire State Building is built on site of the original Waldorf-Astoria Hotel.

The Empire State Building has a public observatory on its 86th floor. The journey from street level takes less than a minute.

During the spring and fall bird migration seasons, the lights that illuminate the Empire State Building tower are turned off on foggy nights so that lights shining through the fog will not confuse birds, causing them to fly into the building.

71

THE DIARIES

DAWN POWELL

July 8

A N EVENING UP on the Empire State roof—the strangest
experience. The huge tomb in steel and glass, the ride
to the 84th floor and there, under the clouds, a Hawaiian
string quartet, lounge, concessions and, a thousand feet
below, New York—a garden of golden lights winking on
and off, automobiles, trucks winding in and out, and not
a sound. All as silent as a dead city—it looks *adagio*
down there.

*T*here is nothing more poetic and terrible than the skyscrapers' battle with the heavens that cover them. Snow, rain, and mist highlight, drench, or conceal the vast towers, but those towers, hostile to mystery and blind to any sort of play, shear off the rain's tresses and shine their three thousand swords through the soft swan of the fog.

—FEDERICO GARCIA LORCA

FORTY-SECOND STREET

WORDS BY AL DUBIN

In the heart of little old New York,
you'll find a thoroughfare.
It's the part of little old New York
that runs into Times Square.

A crazy quilt that "Wall Street Jack"
    built,
if you've got a little time to spare,
I want to take you there.
~~Come and me~~ ... ~~dancing~~ feet,
on the avenue I'm taking you to,
Forty-Second Street.

Hear the beat of dancing feet,
it's the song I love the melody of,
Forty-Second Street.
Little "nifties" from the Fifties,
innocent and sweet;
sexy ladies from the Eighties,
who are indiscreet.

They're side by side,
they're glorified
where the underworld can meet the elite,
Forty-Second Street.

naughty, bawdy, gawdy, sporty,
Forty-Second Street.

77

EVERY DAY, FIFTEEN MINUTES before curtain time, George M. Cohan's "Give My Regards to Broadway" chimes from atop the Paramount Theater in Times Square, alerting theatergoers to rush to their seats. While the Great White Way is home to the largest concentration of theaters in New York, attracting 11 million spectators annually, New York City theater's humble roots began during the Colonial period in Lower Manhattan.

The first recorded theater in New York City was the New Theater, or the Theater in Nassau Street, which staged its first professional performance of Richard III in 1750. Park Theater on Park Row dominated dramatic activity in the early 1800s, welcoming accomplished British actors and presenting Italian operas. The African Theater opened in 1821, and nurtured the career of Ira Aldridge, the first black actor in the United States to gain international recognition. By 1824 theaters were concentrated on Broadway and the Bowery—Broadway catered to the more elite classes, while the Bowery attracted a working-class audience.

Though blackface had been around since late 1700s, Thomas D. "Jim Crow" Rice brought the minstrelsy into the forefront of New York theater in the 1840s. Minstrel shows perpetuated derogatory stereotypes of blacks, making it difficult for them to be accepted as legitimate stage actors. The minstrelsy also caused ethnic discord amongst Americans and British in the city. The Astor Place Riot of 1849 occurred when supporters of the American actor Edwin Forrest interrupted a performance by his English rival, William C. MacCready. Police killed twenty-two and wounded forty-eight people when they fired to disperse the crowd.

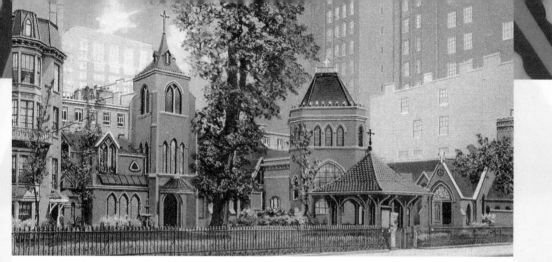

In the mid-19th century, theater had clear-cut class divisions: opera for the upper- and middleclass, minstrel shows and melodramas for the middleclass, and more raunchy variety shows in saloons for working and lower-middleclass men. Entrepreneurs created vaudeville by taking the basic elements of variety and making it more family friendly, which attracted larger audiences and profits. From the 1880s to the 1920s, vaudeville was the most popular form of theater in the U.S., producing performers such as Groucho Marx, Fanny Brice, and James Cagney.

For the first half of the 19th century, theaters clustered around lower Manhattan. In the 1870s Union Square became the first actual theater district where it prospered economically from the need for artists, agents, and printers, as well restaurants and hotels.

In 1870, the distinguished British actor George Holland died, and when the Church of the Atonement refused to conduct services for an "actor," the church around the corner was suggested as an alternative. Entertainers at the

time were generally thought to partake in a dishonorable profession. "Thank God for the Little Church Around the Corner," proclaimed actor Joseph Jefferson, who represented the Holland family. The Church of the Transformation on 29th Street and Fifth Avenue, a.k.a., "The Little Church Around the Corner", has been identified with the theater profession ever since and even depicts actors, rather than saints, on the stained-glass windows.

By the early 1900s, the center of legitimate theater moved uptown to Times Square. The 1920s saw an increase in psychological dramas, giving rise to productions based on the works of Ibsen, Shaw, O'Neill, and Chekov, both on Broadway and in the more experimental theaters of Greenwich Village. The Theater Guild, established in 1914 as the Washington Square Players, provided an alternative to mainstream theater. Vaudeville was going out of fashion in the late 1920s, and was replaced by musicals like *Showboat* and *Porgy and Bess* that addressed more serious topics.

The Depression resulted in unemployment for 5,000 actors and 25,000 theater employees nationwide. The federal government then became a "producer" through its Federal Theater Project, with its largest branch in NYC. It encompassed a Black Theater Wing and a troupe that produced social documentaries. During World War II, theater was dominated by patriotic and escapist dramas, while musical comedies thrived in the 1940s and 1950s. Off-Broadway began in 1952 as a response to the increased conservatism of Broadway audiences, the prohibitive staging costs, and the use of only professional actors. The 1960s brought two instrumental playwrights who shaped NYC theater—Edward Albee and Neil Simon—and also saw the formation of the Negro Ensemble in 1967, which enabled blacks to successfully and dramatically represent black life.

The 1960s also gave rise to Off Off-Broadway theater, as a reaction to the turbulent political climate. Incorporating actors of all races and sexual orientation, it used unconventional theatrical means of expression not necessarily accepted by mainstream audiences. Alternative theater generated some of the most influential playwrights of the 1970s and 1980s including David Mamet and Sam Shepard, who debuted many of their plays in Off-Broadway theaters.

By the 1990s, the cost of a typical Broadway show was $8 million with a successful run of 60–65 weeks needed to reimburse investors. Theater continues to be one of the most popular forms of entertainment and revenue in New York City, with 40 Broadway theaters currently in operation. There are an estimated 150 Off and Off Off-Broadway performance spaces in the five boroughs, producing more than 1,500 performances annually. From 2000–2001, Broadway contributed roughly $4.42 billion to the economy of NYC and supported 40,000 jobs. Through its humble beginnings and radical social transformations, theater has created an empire of sight and sound that continually draws thousands to New York City each day.

BROADWAY

SARA TEASDALE

This is the quiet hour; the theaters
 Have gathered in their crowds, and steadily
 The million lights blaze on for few to see,
Robbing the sky of stars that should be hers.
A woman waits with bag and shabby furs,
 A somber man drifts by, and only we
 Pass up the street unwearied, warm and free,
For over us the olden magic stirs.
Beneath the liquid splendor of the lights
 We live a little ere the charm is spent;
This night is ours, of all the golden nights,
 The pavement an enchanted palace floor,
And Youth the player on the viol, who sent
 A strain of music thru an open door.

THE GREAT WHITE WAY

❈

There are now only four theaters actually situated on Broadway: The Marquis (46th), The Palace (47th), The Winter Garden (50th) and The Broadway (53rd).

❈

Broadway theatres were among the first to wow crowds by using electric bulbs on signs—the bright lights earned the Broadway stretch between 42st and 53rd streets the nickname "The Great White Way."

❈

Longacre Square was renamed Times Square when the *New York Times* Building was erected in 1904.

❈

The Booth Theatre was named after one of America's greatest 19th century classical actors, Edwin Booth (brother of Lincoln assassin John Wilkes Booth).

❈

Mae West's 1926 play *Sex*, about a Montreal prostitute, ran for a year before the city charged the company with lewdness and the corrupting of youth. She spent 10 days in jail.

❈

New York City theaters became desegregated in 1912.

❈

The original production of *The Wizard of Oz* was the premier performance at the Majestic Theatre on January 21, 1903.

❈

Economically, the 1927–28 season is the most successful in the history of New York City theater: 264 shows opened in 76 Broadway theaters.

❈

Before the advent of air conditioning, most theaters closed down during the summer.

The longest running show in Broadway history was *Cats*. It opened at the Winter Garden Theatre in 1982, and didn't close until 2000.

Named Heere Straat (High Street) by the Dutch, Broadway was one of two main trading routes leading north from the tip of lower Manhattan. During the American Revolution, British and American troops traveled and fought along it.

Dustin Hoffman shared a New York City apartment with Gene Hackman while he studied at the Actor's Studio, and worked as a janitor and attendant in a mental hospital.

LOOKING FOR LOVE ON BROADWAY

James Taylor

Need a reason to be here.
Hoping to find it tonight,
Walking alone on Broadway,
Watching the people watching the
    town go down.

Broadway's a river to me;
Fat fish in the big city sea.
Taxi cabs, limousines,
Submarines.

Got my mind on a sweet dream.
Keeping an eye on this street scene,
'Cause I'm open for love in the middle
    of town tonight.
Had my fill of self-pity.

I brought all my blues to the city.
Guess I'm pressin' my luck in the
    middle of town tonight.
See me waiting on you to smile back
    on me, child.

It looks like tomorrow.
It seems like the end of a dream,
Dawning on me on Broadway.

In the morning light, it's a dream.
I'm just a fool looking for love on
    Broadway.

AMERICAN NOTES

CHARLES DICKENS

THE GREAT PROMENADE and thoroughfare, as most people know, is Broadway; a wide and bustling street, which, from the Battery Gardens to its opposite termination in a country road, may be four miles long. Shall we sit down in an upper floor of the Carlton House Hotel (situated in the best part of this main artery of New York), and when we are tired of looking down upon the life below, sally forth arm-in-arm, and mingle with the stream?

Warm weather! The sun strikes upon our heads at this open window, as though its rays were concentrated through a burning-glass; but the day is in its zenith, and the season an unusual one. Was there ever such a sunny street as this Broadway? The pavement stones are polished with the tread of feet until they shine again; the red bricks of the houses might be yet in the dry, hot kilns; and the roofs of those omnibuses look as though, if water were poured on them, they would hiss and smoke, and smell like half-quenched fires. No stint of omnibuses here! Half-a-dozen have gone by within as many minutes....Heaven save the ladies, how they dress! We have seen more colors in these ten minutes, than we should have seen elsewhere, in as many days. What various parasols! what rainbow silks and satins! what pinking of thin stockings, and pinching of thin shoes, and fluttering of ribbons and silk tassels, and display of rich cloaks with gaudy hoods and linings! The young gentlemen are fond, you see, of turning down their shirt-collars and cultivating their whiskers, especially under the chin; but they cannot approach the ladies in their dress or bearing, being, to say the truth, humanity of quite another sort.

KNISH

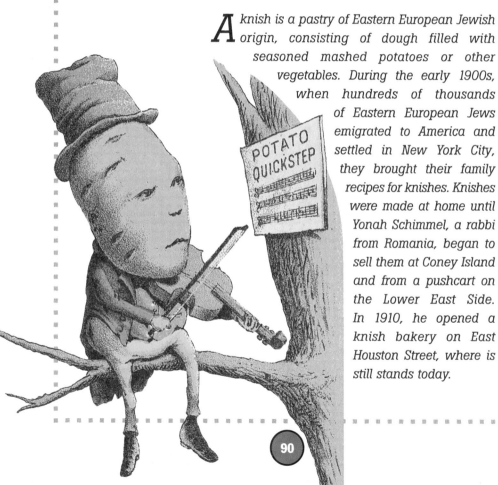

A knish is a pastry of Eastern European Jewish origin, consisting of dough filled with seasoned mashed potatoes or other vegetables. During the early 1900s, when hundreds of thousands of Eastern European Jews emigrated to America and settled in New York City, they brought their family recipes for knishes. Knishes were made at home until Yonah Schimmel, a rabbi from Romania, began to sell them at Coney Island and from a pushcart on the Lower East Side. In 1910, he opened a knish bakery on East Houston Street, where is still stands today.

POTATO QUICKSTEP

KNISH

DOUGH
2 cups all-purpose flour

1/2 teaspoon baking powder

1/4 teaspoon salt

1 egg

1/4 cup vegetable oil

FILLING
2 tablespoons rendered chicken fat (aka: shmatlz), melted (butter can be substituted)

2 tablespoons finely chopped yellow onion

Salt and pepper

4 large Idaho potatoes, cooked and mashed

1 egg, beaten

1. Preheat oven to 375° F.

2. In a large bowl, sift flour, baking powder, and salt. Make a well in the center of the dry ingredients and add egg and oil. Beat liquid ingredients lightly with a fork and gradually stir in the flour mixture by tipping in the edges of the well. Knead until dough is soft. It should be slightly oily, but not sticky.

3. Cover and set in a warm place for 1 hour.

4. For filling, heat chicken fat/shmaltz in a sauté pan over medium-high heat. Add onion and cook until the onion is soft and golden brown. Season with salt and pepper.

5. Combine onions and potatoes. Set aside.

6. On a clean, dry surface, divide the dough in half and roll as thin as possible into a rectangle. Spread the filling on the bottom quarter of long side of the dough and roll like a jelly roll. Cut into 1-inch slices. Pull ends of the dough over the filling and tuck to form small cakes. Place on a well-greased baking sheet.

7. Using a small pastry brush, brush knishes with beaten egg. Bake 25–30 minutes, or until golden brown.

Yields two dozen knishes.

APOLOGY FOR BREATHING

A. J. LIEBLING

SINCE THIS IS A REGIONAL BOOK about people I met back where I came from, I should like to say something here about the local language. This is a regional tongue imported from the British Isles, as is the dialect spoken by the retarded inhabitants of the Great Smoky Mountains back where *they* come from. Being spoken by several million people, it has not been considered of any philological importance. Basically, New Yorkese is the common speech of early nineteenth century Cork, transplanted during the mass immigration of the South Irish a hundred years ago. Of this Cork dialect Thomas Crofton Croker in 1839 wrote: "The vernacular of this region may be regarded as the ancient cockneyism of the mixed race who held the old city—Danes, English and Irish. It is a jargon, whose principal characteristic appears in the pronunciation of *th*, as exemplified in *dis, dat, den, dey*—this, that, then, they; and in the dovetailing of words as, 'kum our rish' for 'come of this.'" New York example, "gerradahere" for "get out of here." The neo-Corkonian proved particularly suited to the later immigrants who

93

came here from continental Europe—the *th* sound is equally impossible for French, Germans and Italians. Moreover, it was impressed upon the latecomers because it was the talk of the police and the elementary school teachers, the only Americans who would talk to them at all. Father, who was born in Austria but came here when he was seven years old, spoke New Yorkese perfectly.

It is true that since the diaspora the modern dialects of Cork and New York have diverged slightly like Italian and Provencal, both of which stem from vulgar Latin. Yet Sean O'Faolain's modern story of Cork, "A Born Genius," contains dialogue that might have come out of Eleventh Avenue: "He's after painting two swans on deh kitchen windes. Wan is facin' wan way an d'oder is facin' d'oder way.—So dat so help me God dis day you'd tink deh swans was floatin' in a garden! And deh garden was floatin' in trough deh winda! And dere was no winda!"

There are interesting things about New York besides the language. It is one of the oldest places in the United States, but doesn't live in retrospect like the professionally picturesque provinces. Any city may have one period of magnificence, like Boston or New Orleans or San Francisco, but it takes a real one to keep renewing itself until the past is perennially forgotten. There were plenty of clipper ships out of New York in the old days and privateers before them, but there are better ships out of here today. The revolution was fought all over town, from Harlem to Red Hook and back again, but that isn't the revolution you will hear New Yorkers discussing now.

Native New Yorkers are the best mannered people in America; they never speak out of turn in saloons, because they have experience in group etiquette. Whenever you hear a drinker let a blat out of him you can be sure he is a recent immigrant from the south or middle west. New Yorkers are modest. It is a distinction for a child in New York to be the brightest on one block; he acquires no exaggerated idea of his own relative intelligence. Prairie geniuses are raced in cheap company when young. They are intoxicated by the feel of being boy wonders in Amarillo, and when they bounce off New York's skin as adults they resent it.

New York women are the most beautiful in the world. They have their teeth straightened in early youth. They get their notions of chic from S. Klein's windows instead of the movies. Really loud and funny New Yorkers, like Bruce Barton, are invariably carpet-baggers. The climate is extremely healthy. The death rate is lower in Queens and the Bronx than in any other large city in the United States, and the average life expectancy is so high that one of our morning newspapers specializes in interviewing people a hundred years old and upward. The average is slightly lowered, however, by the inlanders who come here and insist on eating in Little Southern Tea Roomes on side streets.

NEW YORK, NEW YORK

David Berman

A second New York is being built
a little west of the old one.
Why another, no one asks,
just build it, and they do.

The city is still closed off
to all but the work crews
who claim it's a perfect mirror image.

Truthfully, each man works on the replica
of the apartment building he lived in,
adding new touches,
like cologne dispensers, rock gardens,
and doorknobs marked for the grand hotels.

Improvements here and there, done secretly
and off the books. None of the supervisors
notice or mind. Everyone's in a wonderful mood,
joking, taking walks through the still streets
that the single reporter allowed inside has described as

"unleavened with reminders of the old city's
    complicated past,
but giving off some blue perfume from the early years
    on earth."

The men grow to love the peaceful town.
It becomes more difficult to return home at night,

which sets the wives to worrying.
The yellow soups are cold, the sunsets quick.

The men take long breaks on the fire escapes,
waving across the quiet spaces to other workers
meditating on their perches.

Until one day...

The sky fills with charred clouds.
Toolbelts rattle in the rising wind.

Something is wrong.

A foreman stands in the avenue
pointing binoculars at a massive gray mark
moving towards us in the eastern sky.

Several voices, What, What is it?

Pigeons, he yells through the wind.

A splendid desert—a domed and steepled solitude, where the stranger is lonely in the midst of a million of his race.

—MARK TWAIN

MADE IN NY

The Tootsie Roll was invented in 1896 by an Austrian immigrant, and named for his daughter Clara, whose nickname was Tootsie.

During the Great Depression, unemployed Poughkeepsie architect Alfred Mosher Butts invented the game Lexico, which in 1948 became known as Scrabble®. He studied the front page of *The New York Times* to calculate how often each letter was used. Butts then assigned different point values to each letter and decided how many of each would be included.

Muzak began in New York City in the early 1920s when a retired Army major named George Squier invented a method to broadcast on a telephone line while still allowing telephone calls to go through. He founded a company, later named Muzak—a combination of "music" and "Kodak," then the most popular trade name. Squier's successor redesigned Muzak to be piped into factories to help keep workers happy and productive. Muzak was soon heard in offices, waiting rooms, hotel lobbies, the White House and, of course, elevators.

Joseph C. Gayetty of New York City invented toilet paper in 1857. Before then, people had used pages torn from mail order catalogs, rags, and even leaves. "Gayetty's Medicated Paper" sold in packs of 500 for $.50, claiming it was useful for the "prevention of piles."

On March 9, 1959, Mattel introduced the Barbie doll at the American Toy Fair, held at Manhattan's Toy Center. Based on a German doll called Lilli, Ruth Handler, co-founder of Mattel named the doll after her daughter, Barbara.

In 1912, German immigrant Richard Hellmann introduced Hellmann's Blue Ribbon Mayonnaise at his deli, Hellmann's Delicatessen, on Columbus Avenue. Hellmann used his wife's unique recipe.

Brooklyn-born Clarence Birdseye was a field naturalist in the Arctic when he discovered the fish he caught froze quickly, but tasted fresh when thawed and eaten later. He started the General Seafood Corporation in 1924 and, by 1930, was selling 26 different frozen vegetables, fruits, fish, and meats.

In 1827, Hannah Montague of Troy, New York invented the detachable collar. She was tired of washing her husband's shirts to get the collars clean, so she cut the collars off and washed them separately. The idea caught on and collars became a status symbol for office workers, which is where the term "white collar worker" comes from.

The first mechanized tattoo shop opened in 1875 at 11 Chatham Square by Samuel F. O'Reilly, who invented the electric tattoo machine after observing Thomas Edison's electric engraving pen.

ABSTRACT EXPRESSIONISM was an American art movement in New York City from the mid-1940s to mid-1950s, and was the first specifically American art movement to establish worldwide influence. It demonstrated the energy and creativity of America in the post-World War II years, and was the first important school in American painting to establish its own aesthetic ideals of beauty, independent of European influence. The act of painting was regarded as more significant than the finished products, as painters sought to express their subconscious through art.

Peggy Guggenheim was an instrumental figure in advancing the careers of Abstract Expressionists. Born in 1898 to a wealthy NYC family, her father, Benjamin Guggenheim, died aboard the *Titanic* in 1912, and her uncle, Solomon Guggenheim, established the Solomon R. Guggenheim Foundation and Museum. While living in Paris in the 1920s, she befriended and served as patron to many *avant-garde* writers and artists, and began amassing an impressive collection of modern art. She opened a gallery in London and in 1942 opened the gallery *Art of This Century* in New York.

Peggy Guggenheim's patronage included Jackson Pollock, whom she supported with a monthly stipend while actively promoting and selling his paintings. Pollock's first show was at her gallery. She also held temporary exhibitions of many then-unknown young

American artists such as Robert Motherwell, Mark Rothko, and Clyfford Still. In 1969, the Solomon R. Guggenheim Museum invited Peggy Guggenheim to show her extensive collection of modern art, which she subsequently donated to the Museum's foundation. The Solomon R. Guggenheim Museum, designed by Frank Lloyd Wright, is one of New York City's treasures, housing a vast collection of modern and contemporary art.

Jackson Pollock, Willem de Kooning, and Mark Rothko were among the most celebrated Abstract Expressionists, though their work varied greatly.

- Jackson Pollock (1912–56) arrived in New York City in 1929 to study at the Art Student's League and became recognized as one of the most original painters in America. He was known for his technique of dripping and pouring paint on a canvas laying on the floor. He employed the method referred to as "all-over painting" in which the whole surface of the canvas is treated in a relatively uniform manner, with no set top, bottom, or center.

- Dutch-born Willem de Kooning (1904–97) came to the United States as a stowaway. He became a leader of Abstract Expressionism with a more figurative style. *Woman I* and *Bicycle* were among his most important works, and *Woman I* became one of the most reproduced paintings in the United States. He worked well into his eighties.

- Mark Rothko (1903–1970) was born in Russia and arrived in New York City in 1923, where he studied at the Art Student's League. His paintings feature expanses of color arranged in a vertical format. Despite his success, he was depressed and felt misunderstood by critics; he eventually committed suicide.

By the 1960s, Pop art, color field painting, and minimalism had emerged. One of the most celebrated Pop artists was Andy Warhol, who, after a career as a commercial illustrator in New York in the 1950s, began making Pop imagery and underground films at his studio, known as "The Factory." Most notable were his Campbell's Soup cans and Marilyn Monroe images. Tom Wesselman, Helen Frankenthaler, Robert Rauschenberg, and Saul Steinberg were just a few of the incredible talents to emerge in New York during the second half of the 20th century, firmly establishing New York as the art capitol of the world.

WILLEM DE KOONING REMEMBERS MARK ROTHKO

JOSEPH LISS

...IT WAS IN THE DEPRESSION PERIOD. I had a studio in a loft on Twenty-second Street. So after a day's work I used to hang around Washington Square Park at night. Also we used to sit at the Waldorf Cafeteria. For years the artists had met there, you know, everybody. Rothko didn't come there very often. That's why I didn't know what he looked like. I had never met him. And so one night, in the park, it was late, wasn't a soul around. I walked around—thought I would sit a little bit on a bench. I was sitting way on the right side of the bench and kind of a husky man was on the left end of the bench, and I thought maybe I ought to move and sit on another bench....I didn't know what he was thinking. We were just sitting there—wasn't a soul around. It must have been very late, or otherwise it was just one of those evenings that people didn't show up. And the park was really quite empty. And we just sat there until Mark said something like it was a nice evening. And so I say, "Yes, a nice evening," and we got to talk.

I guess he must have asked me what I did. I said, "I'm a painter." He says, "Oh, you're a painter? I'm a painter, too." And he said, "What's your name?" I said, "I'm Bill de Kooning." I said, "Who are you?" He says, "I'm Rothko." I said, "Oh, for God's sake," and said it was very funny. Then we talked, and a couple of days later he came to visit me in my studio.

PICKLES

*P*icking is one of the oldest methods of preserving food. In the sixteenth century, the Dutch cultivated pickles as a prized delicacy. The area that is now New York City was home to the largest concentration of commercial picklers at the time. By 1659, Dutch farmers in New York grew cucumbers all over what is now Brooklyn and sold them to dealers who cured them in barrels filled with varying flavored brines. By the turn of the twentieth century, there were numerous Eastern European pickle vendors on the Lower East Side. Izzy Guss, who came to New York from Russia, began selling pickles with a pushcart. For almost 100 years customers line up to crunch on these perfectly crispy, juicy treats from Guss' pickle barrels. It is a New York custom for a deli to serve a pickle slice with each sandwich.

The most important thing about this recipe is prepping the jars the pickles will be stored in.

1 24-ounce jar

1 lb. pickling cucumbers

1 cup white vinegar

1 cup water

1/2 cup salt

12 peeled, sliced garlic cloves

1 tablespoon peppercorns

3 tablespoons dill seeds

1. In a large pot, boil enough water to submerge as many jars as you are intending to use. Once at a rolling boil, carefully lower jars and lids completely into the water. Allow to boil in the water bath for ten minutes before carefully removing them. DO NOT use your hands! Use clean tongs! The jars need to be as sanitary as possible (besides, you'd burn yourself).

2. To prepare the pickles, begin by thoroughly washing the cucumbers and cutting them in half lengthwise.

3. Combine vinegar, water, and salt and bring to a boil.

4. Pack the cucumbers and garlic into hot sterilized jars and add peppercorns and dill seeds.

5. Fill the jars with the hot pickling liquid and seal immediately. Jars should be placed upside down as they cool for the first 24 hours.

6. Refrigerate and enjoy. If you take great care when packing the pickles, they will keep for several months.

Makes one 24-ounce jar of pickles.

109

I HAPPEN TO LIKE NEW YORK

Cole Porter

I happen to like New York,
I happen to like this town.
I like the city air,
I like to drink of it,

The more I know New York
the more I think of it.
I like the sight and the sound
and even the stink of it,
I happen to like New York.

I like to go to Battery park
And watch those liners booming in.
I often ask myself, why should it be
That they should come so far from
   across the sea,
I suppose it's because they all agree
   with me,
They happen to like New York.

Last Sunday afternoon
I took a trip to Hackensack,
But after I gave Hackensack the
   once over,
I took the next train back.
I happen to like New York,
I happen to love this burg.

And when I have to give the world
   a last farewell,
And the undertaker starts to ring my
   fun'ral bell,
I don't want to go to heaven,
don't want to go to hell
I happen to like New York,
I happen to like New York.

THE NEW COLOSSUS

Emma Lazarus

Not like the brazen giant of Greek fame,
With conquering limbs astride from land to land;
Here at our sea-washed, sunset gates shall stand
A might woman with a torch, whose flame
is the imprisoned lightning, and her name
Mother of Exiles. From her beacon-hand
Glows the world-wide welcome; her mild eyes command
The air-bridged harbor that twin cities frame.
"Keep ancient lands, your storied pomp!" cries she
With silent lips. "Give me your tired, your poor,
Your huddled masses yearning to breathe free,
The wretched refuse of your teeming shore.
Send these, the homeless, tempest-lost to me,
I lift my lamp beside the golden door!"

*I*t can destroy an individual, or it can fulfill him, depending a good deal on luck. No one should come to New York to live unless he is willing to be lucky.

—E. B. WHITE

"LA LIBERTÉ ÉCLAIRANT LE MONDE" or "Liberty Enlightening the World" is the name given to the Statue the Liberty by its sculptor, Frederic Auguste Bartholdi. In recognition of the friendship established during the American Revolution, French statesman Edouard de Laboulaye proposed presenting a monument to America as a gift from the people of France, symbolizing freedom to the entire world. The statue was a joint effort between the two countries—Americans would build the pedestal and the French would build the statue—in honor of the centennial of the Declaration of Independence.

Bartholdi was commissioned to design the sculpture and Gustave Eiffel created Lady Liberty's skeleton—four huge iron columns supporting a metal framework holding the thin copper skin. Bartholdi chose copper because it was attractive, yet durable enough to withstand the long voyage, and virtually impervious to the salt-laden air of New York Harbor. He first created the statue's right arm and torch, which were exhibited at Philadelphia's Centennial Exposition in 1876 and then displayed in Madison Square Park to raise funds for the construction of the statue's pedestal. The financing of the pedestal was completed in August 1885 and construction was finished in April 1886.

Completed in France, the statue arrived in New York in June of 1885 in 350 pieces. Reassembling it took four months and the statue was placed upon a granite pedestal on what is now known as Liberty Island. On October 28th 1886, a decade after the centennial, President Grover Cleveland unveiled and dedicated the Statue of Liberty, to thousands of spectators. In 1903, Emma Lazarus' poem, "The New Colossus"—*"Give me your tired, your poor, your huddled masses yearning to breathe free..."*—was inscribed on a bronze tablet laid in the statue's pedestal.

QUICK FACTS ABOUT THE STATUE:

- The statue—151 feet, 1 inch tall—was the tallest structure in the U.S. at the time she was erected.

- In 50 m.p.h winds she sways 3 inches from side to side; her torch sways 5 inches.

- There are 25 windows in her crown, which symbolize gemstones found on the earth and the heaven's light shining over the world.

- The seven rays of the Statue's crown represent the seven seas and continents of the world.

- Visitors must climb 354 steps to see the vistas from the crown.

- The tablet, which the Statue holds in her left hand, reads "July 4th, 1776" in Roman numerals.

- The statue is covered in 300 sheets of copper, $3/32$ of an inch thick.

- Lady Liberty's shoe size is 879 (Women's, U.S.)

THE GREAT GATSBY

F. SCOTT FITZGERALD

I BEGAN TO LIKE NEW YORK, the racy, adventurous feel of it at night, and the satisfaction that the constant flicker of men and women and machines gives to the restless eye. I liked to walk up Fifth Avenue and pick out romantic women from the crowd and imagine that in a few minutes I was going to enter into their lives, and no one would ever know or disapprove. Sometimes, in my mind, I followed them to their apartments on the corners of hidden streets, and they turned and smiled back to me before they faded through a door into warm darkness. At the enchanted metropolitan twilight I felt a haunting loneliness sometimes, and felt it in others—poor young clerks who loitered in front of windows waiting until it was time for a solitary restaurant dinner—young clerks in the dusk, wasting the most poignant moments of night and life.

Again at eight o'clock, when the dark lanes of the Forties were five deep with throbbing taxicabs bound for the theater district, I felt a sinking in my heart. Forms leaned together in the taxis as they waited, and voices sang, and there was laughter from unheard jokes, and lighted cigarettes outlined unintelligible gestures inside. Imagining that I, too, was hurrying toward gayety and sharing their intimate excitement, I wished them well.

WALDORF SALAD

1 1/2 cups apple, chopped (traditionally a Red Delicious— the New York apple— however, if you prefer, use Granny Smith, Pippin or a combination of different apples)

1 tablespoon lemon juice

1 cup celery, chopped

1/4 cup mayonnaise

1/4 cup raisins, soaked in boiling water 20 minutes

1/4 cup walnuts, chopped

Waldorf salad was created at New York's Waldorf-Astoria Hotel in the 1890s. The original version of this salad contained only apples, celery, and mayonnaise. A decade later, chopped walnuts became an integral part of the dish. Waldorf salad is usually served on a bed of lettuce. The dish has become a staple for "ladies who lunch."

1. Toss apples with lemon juice after they are cut to prevent discoloration.

2. Add all other ingredients. Toss to coat everything with mayonnaise. Serve.

PARKS

New York City has more than 1,700 parks, playgrounds, and recreation facilities across the five boroughs.

Brooklyn's Prospect Park is considered to be the masterpiece of architect/designers Frederick Law Olmstead and Calvert Vaux. Central Park, however, gets more attention.

The New York Botanical Garden is home to the nation's largest Victorian glasshouse, the Enid A. Haupt Conservatory. This New York City landmark has showcased the garden's distinguished tropical, Mediterranean, and desert plant collections since 1902.

Sonnenberg Gardens in Canandaigua has nine formal gardens and one of the largest displays of roses in the state.

The northern end of Central Park was the site of a series of fortifications for the Revolutionary War and the War of 1812.

Central Park's original carousel, built 1871, was turned by "horsepower." Twice destroyed by fire, it was replaced by the current brick structure in 1951.

A tree may grow in Brooklyn, but there are 26,000 growing in Central Park. When the park was first under construction in the early 1850s, the quality of the soil was so poor that 500,000 cubic feet of topsoil had to be carted in from New Jersey.

There are 800 species of birds in North America—275 of them can be seen in Central Park.

All the pedestrian paths in Central Park add up to 58 miles.

Central Park hosts 25 million visitors a year–250,000 on a spring weekend.

Central Park's Mall, culminating at Bethesda Terrace, was envisioned by Olmsted and Vaux as the "grand promenade" for park visitors to see and be seen. It was the only formal architectural design element in the park.

Since 1908, more than 175 movies have contained scenes in Central Park.

In 1961 and 1965 respectively, the Metropolitan Opera and the New York Philharmonic began giving free concerts in the park. Shakespeare in the Park started in 1962.

SKETCHES FROM LIFE

LEWIS MUMFORD

Y ES: I LOVED THE GREAT BRIDGES and walked back and forth
over them, year after year. But as often happens with repeated
experiences, one memory stands out above all others: a
twilight hour in early spring—it was March, I think—when, starting
from the Brooklyn end, I faced into the west wind sweeping over
the rivers from New Jersey. The ragged, slate-blue cumulus
clouds that gathered over the horizon left open patches for the
light of the waning sun to shine through, and finally, as I reached
the middle of the Brooklyn Bridge, the sunlight spread across the
sky, forming a halo around the jagged mountain of skyscrapers,
with the darkened loft buildings and warehouses huddling below
in the foreground. The towers, topped by the golden pinnacles
of the new Woolworth Building, still caught the light even as it
began to ebb away. Three-quarters of the way across the Bridge
I saw the skyscrapers in the deepening darkness become slowly
honeycombed with lights until, before I reached the Manhattan
end, these buildings piled up in a dazzling mass against the
indigo sky.

Here was my city, immense, overpowering, flooded with energy
and light; there below lay the river and the harbor, catching the
last flakes of gold on their waters, with the black tugs, free from
their barges, plodding dockward, the ferry boats lumbering

from pier to pier, the tramp steamers slowly crawling toward the sea, the Statue of Liberty erectly standing, little curls of steam coming out of boat whistles or towered chimneys, while the rumbling elevated trains and trolley cars just below me on the bridge moved in a relentless tide to carry tens of thousands homeward. And there was I, breasting the March wind, drinking in the city and the sky, both vast, yet both contained in me, transmitting through me the great mysterious will that had made them and the promise of the new day that was still to come.

A TREE GROWS IN BROOKLYN

BETTY SMITH

SERENE WAS A WORD you could put to Brooklyn, New York. Especially in the summer of 1912. Somber, as a word, was better. But it did not apply to Williamsburg, Brooklyn. Prairie was lovely and Shenandoah had a beautiful sound, but you couldn't fit those words into Brooklyn. Serene was the only word for it; especially on a Saturday afternoon in summer.

Late in the afternoon the sun slanted down into the mossy yard belonging to Francie Nolan's house, and warmed the worn wooden fence. Looking at the shafted sun, Francie had that same fine feeling that came when she recalled the poem they recited in school.

> This is the forest primeval. The murmuring pines and the hemlocks,
>
> Bearded with moss, and in garments green, indistinct in the twilight,
>
> Stand like Druids of eld.

The one tree in Francie's yard was neither a pine nor a hemlock. It had pointed leaves which grew along green switches which radiated from the bough and made a tree like a lot of opened green umbrellas. Some people called it the Tree of Heaven. No matter where its seed fell, it made a tree which struggled to reach the sky. It grew in boarded-up lots and out of neglected rubbish heaps and it was the only tree that grew out of cement. It grew lushly, but only in the tenement districts.

You took a walk on a Sunday afternoon and came to a nice neighborhood, very refined. You saw a small one of these trees through the iron gate leading to someone's yard and you knew that soon that section of Brooklyn would get to be a tenement district. The tree knew. It came there first.

BROOKLYN BRIDGE

Though the idea of a bridge from Brooklyn to Manhattan was proposed as far back as 1802, it was the harsh winter of 1866–67 which halted ferry traffic and forced people to walk across the frozen river that finally got the ball rolling. President Grant signed the bill approving construction in 1869.

It took 13 years to build, beginning in 1870. It opened on May 24, 1883.

Architect John A. Roebling died following an accident surveying the site in 1869. His son, Washington, took over for him, but became ill and had to supervise from his bedroom.

Twenty-seven men died during the bridge's construction.

The Brooklyn Bridge was the first bridge to be lit using electricity.

Initially, cable cars "ferried" people across the bridge for a nickel a ride and pedestrians paid a penny to stroll across the promenade. By 1910, the tolls were repealed and crossing the bridge was free.

The Brooklyn Bridge cost $15.1 million to build, more than twice the $7 million estimate. Of that, $3.8 million was used to purchase land for its approaches. The remainder went toward construction.

P. T. Barnum demonstrated the safety of the bridge in 1884 by parading across it with a herd of twenty-one elephants.

Robert E. Odlum became the first man to jump off the bridge in 1885, but did not survive the fall. Clara McArthur became the first woman in 1895. She lived.

On the Brooklyn Bridge, an airplane can fly over a pedestrian who's walking over a car that's driving over a boat that's sailing over a train. (The subway runs under the East River.)

New York is the only real city-city.
—TRUMAN CAPOTE

NEW YORK STRIP STEAK

New York strip steak, approx. 1–1 1/2 lbs.

Coarse sea salt (only use Kosher if your in a desperate pinch and just make something else if all you have in the house is iodized salt)

1 teaspoon black pepper, coarsely ground

2 tablespoons Worcestershire sauce

1 teaspoon Colman's dry mustard

1/2 teaspoon garlic powder

1 teaspoon chili oil (less if desired)

*N*ew York strip steak is more of a connotation than an actual designation of meat. Before refrigeration, the best cuts of beef were reportedly sent to New York City. New York steak came to mean the best steak that tended to be well-marbled and top grade, which came from strong, well-developed cattle. In general, it is 1 to 1 1/4 inches thick and is cut from the center portion of the cow, behind the short rib, where there is little muscle and high fat content. It's basically equivalent to a porterhouse steak minus tenderloin and bone. New York strip is also known as shell steak, strip steak, Kansas City strip, and sirloin club steak.

1. Preheat oven to broil.

2. Using either a fork or a small knife, stab steak numerous times to create tiny perforations.

3. Coat both sides of steak with coarse sea salt. Allow to sit for 5 minutes.

4. Combine all other ingredients and rub generously over steak.

5. Broil for 3–5 minutes per side (for medium rare), basting steak every few minutes with juices that collect in pan.

6. Allow to rest for a few minutes, then slice thin against the grain and serve.

Serves two.

THE DIARIES
GEORGE TEMPLETON STRONG

[1865] MARCH 18 Very energetic in Wall Street. Walked off with George Anthon at two, crossed at Wall Street ferry, and explored sundry new districts of Brooklyn. Visited "Fort Greene," a noble public square with fine views in every direction. I hereby prophesy that in 1900 A.D. Brooklyn will be the city and New York will be the suburb. It is inevitable if both go on growing as they have grown for the last forty years. Brooklyn has room to spread and New York has not. The New Yorker of Thirty-fifth Street already finds it a tedious and annoying job to make his way downtown to business and home again. How will the New Yorker of One-hundredth Street get about forty years hence? Brooklyn must out number this city before very many years, and then places of amuse-ment and fashionable residences will begin to emigrate

across the East River. New York will become "the city" in the London sense of that word. Its Belgravia will be transferred from the Fifth Avenue to King's County. A like change is within my own memory. When I was a boy, the aristocracy lived around the Battery, on the Bowling Green, and in the western streets below Chambers; in Wall Street, Cedar Street, and Beekman Street, on the east of the town. Greenwich Street, now a hissing and a desolation, a place of lager beer saloons, emigrant boarding houses, and the vilest dens, was what Madison Avenue is now. There were the Griswolds in Chambers Street, Philip Hone in Broadway below Park Place, Mrs. Cruger at No. 55, and so on. Between 1828 and 1832, emigration to the regions of Fourth Street, Bond Street, and Lafayette Place set in, and the centres of fashion were moved again, for we are a nomadic people, and our finest brownstone houses are merely tents of new pattern and material. Brooklyn has advantages, too, that will speed the change. The situations on the Heights overlooking the bay can hardly be matched in any great city of Christendom. How often have I wished I could exchange this house for one of them, and that I could see from my library windows that noble prospect and that wide open expanse of sky, and the going down of the sun every evening!

BLACK SPRING

HENRY MILLER

I AM A PATRIOT—of the 14th Ward Brooklyn, where I was raised. The rest of the United States doesn't exist for me, except as idea, or history, or literature. At ten years of age I was uprooted from my native soil and removed to a cemetery, a *Lutheran* cemetery, where the tomb-stones were always in order and the wreaths never faded.

But I was born in the street and raised in the street. "The post-mechanical open street where the most beautiful and hallucinating iron vegetation," etc....Born under the sign of Aries which gives a fiery, active, energetic and somewhat restless body. *With Mars in the ninth house!*

To be born in the street means to wander all your life, to be free. It means accident and incident, drama, movement. It means above all dream. A harmony of irrelevant facts which gives to your wandering a metaphysical certitude.

In the street you learn what human beings really are; otherwise, or afterwards, you invent them. What is not in the open street is false, derived, that is to say, *literature*. Nothing of what is called "adventure" ever approaches the flavor of the street. It doesn't matter whether you fly to the Pole, whether you sit on the floor of the ocean with a pad in your hand, whether you pull up nine cities one after the other, or whether, like Kurtz, you sail up the river and go mad. No matter how exciting, how intolerable the situation, there are always exits, always ameliorations, comforts, compensations, newspapers, religions. But once there was none of this. Once you were free, wild, murderous…

The boys you worshipped when you first came down into the street remain with you all your life. They are the only real heroes. Napoleon, Lenin, Capone—all fiction. Napoleon is nothing to me in comparison with Eddie

Carney, who gave me my first black eye. No man I have ever met seems as princely, as regal, as noble, as Lester Reardon who, by the mere act of walking down the street, inspired fear and admiration. Jules Verne never led me to the places that Stanley Borowski had up his sleeve when it came dark. Robinson Crusoe lacked imagination in comparison with Johnny Paul. All these boys of the 14th Ward have a flavor about them still. They were not invented or imagined: they were real. Their names ring out like gold coins—Tom Fowler, Jim Buckley, Matt Owen, Rob Ramsay, Harry Martin, Johnny Dunne, to say nothing of Eddie Carney or the great Lester Reardon. Why, even now when I say Johnny Paul the names of the saints leave a bad taste in my mouth. Johnny Paul was the living Odyssey of the 14th Ward; that he later became a truck driver is an irrelevant fact.

"TAXIS TOOT WHIRL PEOPLE MOVING"

e. e. cummings

taxis toot whirl people moving perhaps laugh into the slowly
millions and finally O it is spring since at all windows
microscopic birds sing fiercely two ragged men and a
filthiest woman busily are mending three wholly broken somehow
bowls or somethings by the web curb and carefully spring is
somehow skilfully everywhere mending smashed minds
O
the massacred gigantic world
again,into keen sunlight who lifts
glittering selfish new
limbs
and my heart stirs in his rags shaking from his armpits the
abundant lice of dreams laughing

rising sweetly out of the alive new mud my old
man heart striding shouts whimpers screams breathing into
his folded belly acres of sticky sunlight chatters bellows
swallowing globs of big life pricks wickedly his
mangled ears blinks into worlds of colour shrieking
O begins

        the mutilated huge earth
again,up through darkness leaping
who sprints weirdly from its deep prison
groaning with perception and suddenly in all filthy alert things
which jumps mightily out of death
muscular,stinking,erect,entirely born.

HEY, TAXI!

John Hertz, who founded the Yellow Cab Company in 1907, chose yellow for the cabs because he had read a study conducted by the University of Chicago that indicated it was the easiest color to spot.

Yellow became the uniform color for all cabs in 1969 to distinguish them from "gypsy" cabs.

There are 40,000 licensed taxi drivers and 12,187 licensed taxicabs in New York City.

Metered taxis first hit New York City streets on October 1, 1907.

Passengers pay well over $1 billion in fares and tips each year.

Manhattan adults hail a cab an average of 100 times a year.

Nearly half of all customer complaints filed against cabbies involve driver rudeness.

On an average day, drivers serve 30 fares, travel 141 miles, and gross $190 in fares and tips.

Cabs use up about one-third of their miles cruising for fares.

About 400 new drivers
are licensed each month.

89% of new drivers are immigrants.
They come from 84 countries and
speak 60 languages. Nearly half are
from Pakistan, Bangladesh, and India.

Women make up 1.1%
of all licensed drivers.

Approximately 3,670 taxicabs are driven
by the medallion owner. Of these,
20% are leased to a second driver for a
second shift. Most other cabs leased to
two drivers on a double-shift basis.

The current form of medallion number
(e.g., 1A23) was adopted in 1965.
Before 1965, taxicabs were assigned a
new sequential number each year.

SEINLANGUAGE

JERRY SEINFELD

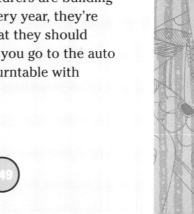

People will kill each other for a parking space in New York because they think, "If I don't get this one, I may never get a space. I'll be searching for months until somebody goes out to the Hamptons." Because everybody in New York City knows there's way more cars than parking spaces. You see cars driving in New York all hours of the night. It's like musical chairs except everybody sat down around 1964.

The problem is, while car manufacturers are building hundreds of thousands of new cars every year, they're not making any new spaces. That's what they should be working on. Wouldn't that be great, you go to the auto show and they've got a big revolving turntable with nothing on it.

"New from Chrysler, a space."

THE SIDEWALKS OF NEW YORK

Chas. B. Lawlor and James W. Blake

Down in front of Casey's,
Old brown wooden stoop,
On a summer's evening,
We formed a merry group;

Boys and girls together,
We would sing and waltz,
While the "Ginnie" played the organ
On the sidewalks of New York.

East side,
West side,
All around the town,
The tots sang "ring a rosie,"
"London Bridge is falling down;"

Boys and girls together,
Me and Mamie Rorke,

Tripped the light fantastic,
On the sidewalks of New York,

That's where Johnny Casey,
And little Jimmy Crowe,
With Jakey Krause the baker,
Who always had the dough,

Pretty Nellie Shannon,
With a dude as light as cork,
First picked up the waltz step
On the sidewalks of New York.

East side,
West side,
All around the town,
The tots sang "ring a rosie,"
"London Bridge is falling down;"

Things have changed since those
    times,
Some are up in "G,"
Others they are wand'rers.
But they all feel just like me,

They would part with all they've got
Could they but once more walk,
With their best girl and have a twirl,
On the sidewalks of New York.

East side,
West side,
All around the town,
The tots sang "ring a rosie,"
"London Bridge is falling down."

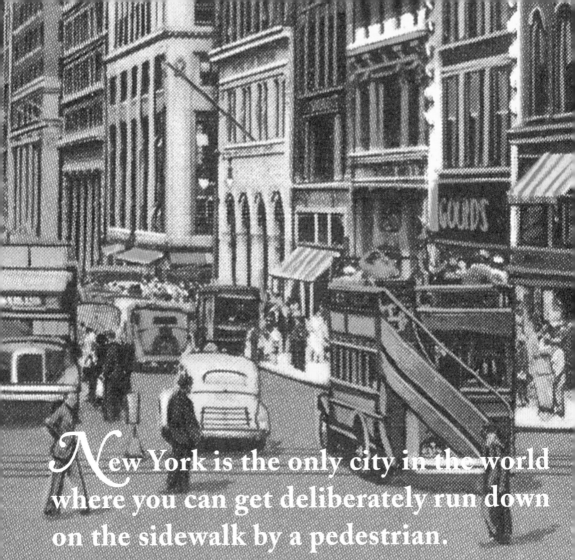

New York is the only city in the world where you can get deliberately run down on the sidewalk by a pedestrian.

—RUSSELL BAKER

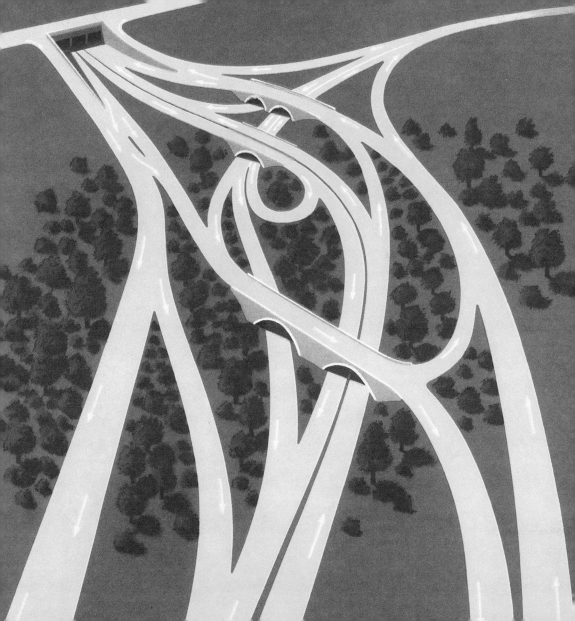

BECAUSE NEW YORK CITY IS virtually an archipelago (only the Bronx connects to the mainland) with more than 500 miles of shoreline, a highly developed system of transportation was instrumental in creating the expansive residential and commercial city we know today. Bridges, tunnels, railroads, and subways were built to transport people without adding to the congestion of the already overcrowded city streets. As a result, crowds were able to travel to farther reaches of the city, experience different cultures, and establish hundreds of thriving communities.

Local public transportation debuted in America in 1827 when a twelve-seat stagecoach began operating along Broadway from the Battery to Bleecker Street. In 1831 the omnibus, a horse-drawn vehicle, was introduced in Manhattan. In 1832 the nation's first railroad, a horse-drawn streetcar line, was constructed.

Until the end of the 19th century, traffic in New York City was largely uncontrolled. Getting across a busy street was quite a challenge, competing with carriages and wagons in every direction. The constant hazard to pedestrians led to the formation of the Broadway Squad in the 1860s, the first traffic-related unit in the NYPD. Officers of the Broadway Squad were the largest and most imposing in the police department, standing a minimum of six feet tall, and their main responsibility was to escort pedestrians safely across Broadway between Bowling Green and West 59th Street.

While ferries existed in the form of rafts and canoes among the original Native American inhabitants of NYC, the Union Ferry Company consolidated a number of competing lines in 1954 and was making 1,250 East River crossings a day; by 1860, it made over 100,000 a day. The opening of the Brooklyn Bridge in 1883 had drastic effects on commuter ferry service. By 1925, all East River ferries ceased operation. The Staten Island ferry is one of the few remaining ferries, and transports about 70,000 passengers a day.

The city's first elevated railways, known as the "els," began service in 1870. They were created as an alternative to streetcars. Though they became a necessity, els were also a public nuisance—they were noisy and caused surrounding buildings to shake. Those underneath them feared being hit by fallen objects, ash, and oil. Mayor LaGuardia eliminated els in the 1930s, to raise the property values of areas along the tracks.

In 1898 the five boroughs united to form New York City. At that time the Brooklyn Bridge was the only physical connection between Brooklyn and Manhattan. Between 1903 and 1909, the Williamsburg, Manhattan, and Queensborough Bridges were constructed across the East River. Seventy-six of New York's 2,027 bridges were constructed across New York City's waterways.

Prior to the official subway opening on October 27, 1904, the inventor and editor of *Scientific American*, Alfred Beach, built a pneumatic subway in 1870, using his own funds. He obtained a permit for a pneumatic tube to carry mail below street level, and secretly built a 312-foot subway under Broadway. Within a year, 400,000 people rode it, paying 25 cents each. Lack of legislative and financial support caused it to close, but Beach's pneumatic subway is considered the prototype for the first city subway, a 9.1-mile long line, consisting of 28 stations from City Hall to 145th Street and Broadway. Service was extended to the Bronx in 1905, to Brooklyn in 1908, and to Queens in 1915. It carried 600,000 passengers per day in its first year. By 1913, the city's rapid transit system carried 810 million passengers, and by 1930, 2,049 million. New York

City's subway system, while not the first, was a technological trendsetter. It was the only four-track system, with express and local trains in both directions, and by World War II carried roughly twice as many passengers than any other system in the world. The subway changed the way people lived, and where they lived. Today, the subway carries more than 7 million passengers a day, and 1.3 billion riders a year.

Yellow taxis have been a visual icon for NYC for decades, but the original cab in 1834 was a horse-driven Hansom cab. Taxicabs became a popular mode of transportation in 1907, when gas-powered vehicles replaced slower-moving vehicles powered by 800-pound batteries. In 1923 there were a total of 15,000 Checker Cabs in NYC. There was an oversupply after the Depression and the 1937 Haas Act capped the number of active licenses. After World War II, the cap made it difficult to meet the city's growing transportation needs and neighborhood car services, or liveries, began to operate in lower-income neighborhoods. The number of livery cars increased from 2,500 in 1964 to over 40,000 today. That's compared to about 12,000 licensed taxis. In 1999, Sotheby's auctioned off New York's last in-service Checker Cab for $134,500—the mileage was 994,050. Over 200 million people use city cabs each year.

New York City's transportation industry not only provided a means of getting from one place to another, but also created thousands of jobs for Americans and immigrants. The city is largely recognized for its transportation—bright yellow taxis, the loud and exciting subway, and the Staten Island Ferry. To get a true taste of the culture and diversity of New York City, just ride the subway, or simply walk down a city street, and observe—the people are what define New York City.

HISTORY OF THE UNITED STATES OF AMERICA DURING THE ADMINISTRATIONS OF THOMAS JEFFERSON

HENRY ADAMS

F WASHINGTON IRVING WAS RIGHT, Rip Van Winkle, who woke from his long slumber about the year 1800, saw little that was new to him, except the head of President Washington where that of King George had once hung, and strange faces instead of familiar ones. Except in numbers, the city was relatively no farther advanced than the country. Between 1790 and 1800 its population rose from 33,000 to 60,000; and if Boston resembled an old-fashioned English market-town, New York was like a foreign seaport, badly paved, undrained, and as foul as a town surrounded by the tides could be. Although the Manhattan Company was laying

wooden pipes for a water supply, no sanitary regulations were enforced, and every few years—as in 1798 and 1803—yellow fever swept away crowds of victims, and drove the rest of the population, panic stricken, into the highlands. No day-police existed; constables were still officers of the courts; the night-police consisted of two captains, two deputies, and seventy-two men. The estimate for the city's expenses in 1800 amounted to $130,000. One marked advantage New York enjoyed over Boston, in the possession of a city government able to introduce reforms. Thus, although still mediaeval in regard to drainage and cleanliness, the town had taken advantage of recurring fires to rebuild some of the streets with brick sidewalks and curbstones. Travelers dwelt much on this improvement, which only New York and Philadelphia had yet adopted, and Europeans agreed that both had the air of true cities: that while Boston was the Bristol of America, New York was the Liverpool, and Philadelphia the London....

The city of New York was so small as to make extravagance difficult; the Battery was a fashionable walk, Broadway a country drive, and Wall Street an uptown residence. Great accumulations of wealth had hardly begun. The Patroon was still the richest man in the State. John Jacob Astor was a fur-merchant living where the Astor House afterward stood, and had not yet begun those purchases of real estate which secured his fortune. Cornelius Vanderbilt was a boy six years old, playing about his father's ferry-boat at Staten Island. New York city itself was what it had been for a hundred years past—a local market.

New York remains what it has always been: a city of ebb and flow, a city of constant shifts of population and economics, a city of virtually no rest. It is harsh, dirty, and dangerous, it is whimsical and fanciful, it is beautiful and soaring—it is not one or another of these things but all of them, all at once, and to fail to accept this paradox is to deny the reality of city existence.

—PAUL GOLDBERGER

THE IMMENSE JOURNEY

LOREN EISELEY

NEW YORK IS NOT, on the whole, the best place to enjoy the downright miraculous nature of the planet. There are, I do not doubt, many remarkable stories to be heard there and many strange sights to be seen, but to grasp a marvel fully it must be savored from all aspects. This cannot be done while one is being jostled and hustled along a crowded street. Nevertheless, in any city there are true wildernesses where a man can be alone. It can happen in a hotel room, or on the high roofs at dawn.

One night on the twentieth floor of a midtown hotel I awoke in the dark and grew restless. On an impulse I climbed upon the broad old-fashioned window sill, opened the curtains and peered out. It was the hour just before dawn, the hour when men sigh in their sleep, or, if awake, strive to focus their wavering eyesight upon a world emerging from the shadows. I leaned out sleepily through the open window. I had expected depths, but not the sight I saw.

I found I was looking down from that great height into a series of curious cupolas or lofts that I could just barely make out in the

darkness. As I looked, the outlines of these lofts became more distinct because the light was being reflected from the wings of pigeons who, in utter silence, were beginning to float outward upon the city. In and out through the open slits in the cupolas passed the white-winged birds on their mysterious errands. At this hour the city was theirs, and quietly, without the brush of a single wing tip against stone in that high, eerie place, they were taking over the spires of Manhattan. They were pouring upward in a light that was not yet perceptible to human eyes, while far down in the black darkness of the alleys it was still midnight.

As I crouched half asleep across the sill, I had a moment's illusion that the world had changed in the night, as in some immense snowfall, and that if I were to leave, it would have to be as these other inhabitants were doing, by the window. I should have to launch out into that great bottomless void with the simple confidence of young birds reared high up there among the familiar chimney pots and interposed horrors of the abyss.

I leaned farther out. To and fro went the white wings, to and fro. There were no sounds from any of them. They knew man was asleep and this light for a little while was theirs. Or perhaps I had only dreamed about man in this city of wings—which he could surely never have built. Perhaps I, myself, was one of these birds dreaming unpleasantly a moment of old dangers far below as I teetered on a window ledge.

Around and around went the wings. It needed only a little courage, only a little shove from the window ledge to enter that city of light. The muscles of my hands were already making little premonitory lunges. I wanted to enter that city and go away over the roofs in the first dawn. I wanted to enter it so badly that I drew back carefully into the room and opened the hall door. I found my coat on the chair, and it slowly became clear to me that there was a way down through the floors, that I was, after all, only a man.

I dressed then and went back to my own kind, and I have been rather more than usually careful ever since not to look into the city of light. I had seen, just once, man's greatest creation from a strange inverted angle, and it was not really his at all. I will never forget how those wings went round and round, and how, by the merest pressure of the fingers and a feeling for air, one might go away over the roofs. It is a knowledge, however, that is better kept to oneself. I think of it sometimes in such a way that the wings, beginning far down in the black depths of the mind, begin to rise and whirl till all the mind is lit by their spinning, and there is a sense of things passing away, but lightly, as a wing might veer over an obstacle.

STEPS

FRANK O'HARA

How funny you are today New York
like Ginger Rogers in *Swingtime*
and St. Bridget's steeple leaning a little to the left

here I have just jumped out of a bed full of V-days
(I got tired of D-days) and blue you there still
accepts me foolish and free
all I want is a room up there
and you in it
and even the traffic halt so thick is a way
for people to rub up against each other
and when their surgical appliances lock
they stay together
for the rest of the day (what a day)
I go by to check a slide and I say
that painting's not so blue

where's Lana Turner
she's out eating
and Garbo's backstage at the Met
everyone's taking their coat off
so they can show a rib-cage to the rib-watchers
and the park's full of dancers and their tights and shoes
in little bags

who are often mistaken for worker-outers at the West Side Y
why not
the Pittsburgh Pirates shout because they won
and in a sense we're all winning
we're alive

the apartment was vacated by a gay couple
who moved to the country for fun
they moved a day too soon
even the stabbings are helping the population explosion
though in the wrong country
and all those liars have left the U N
the Seagram Building's no longer rivaled in interest
not that we need liquor (we just like it)

and the little box is out on the sidewalk
next to the delicatessen
so the old man can sit on it and drink beer
and get knocked off it by his wife later in the day
while the sun is still shining

oh god it's wonderful
to get out of bed
and drink too much coffee
and smoke too many cigarettes
and love you so much

BLACK AND WHITE COOKIES

*S*ince the 1940s the black and white cookie has been a fixture in New York City bakeries and delis. Sometimes referred to as a "half moon," this oversized treat is a cross between a cake and a cookie. They are slightly domed in the center and are frosted half with vanilla icing and half with either chocolate fondant or ganache. The cookie had its 15 (or more) minutes of fame when it appeared in a Seinfeld episode about race relations: "If people would only look to the cookie, all our problems would be solved."

COOKIE DOUGH
1 ¾ cups granulated sugar
1 cup (2 sticks) unsalted butter, softened
4 large eggs
1 cup milk
½ teaspoon vanilla extract
¼ teaspoon lemon extract
2 ½ cups cake flour
2 ½ cups all-purpose flour
1 teaspoon baking powder
½ teaspoon salt

FROSTING
6 cups confectioners' sugar
½ cup boiling water
1 tablespoon vanilla extract
2 ounces bittersweet chocolate

1. Preheat oven to 375° F. Butter two large cookie sheets and set aside.

2. In a large mixing bowl, combine the sugar and butter. Cream until light. Add the eggs, one at a time, followed by the milk, vanilla, and lemon extracts.

3. In a medium bowl, combine the flours, baking powder, and salt.

4. Slowly add the dry ingredients to the wet, stirring just enough to combine everything before making another addition.

BLACK AND WHITE COOKIES

5. Drop large, rounded spoonfuls of the dough two inches apart on the baking sheets. Bake until the edges JUST begin to brown, 20 to 30 minutes, depending on your oven. They should still be springy when pressed underneath. Rotate baking sheets with batches of cookies until the dough is gone. Allow to cool completely.

6. To make the frosting, place the confectioners' sugar in a large bowl. Gradually add the boiling water to the sugar. You may need to vary the amount of water you use depending on the climate, the day, or your mood, so always add the water slowly.

7. Watching for consistency, stir constantly, until the mixture is thick and spreadable. (If you add too much water, just add more sugar until you get the right balance.) If you want a shinier frosting, add a few drops of vegetable oil. Divide the frosting into two bowls. Add vanilla to one and set aside.

8. Melt the chocolate in a double boiler set over simmering water. Add the other half of frosting and stir until smooth. Remove from heat.

9. Using a clean pastry brush, coat half the cookie with chocolate frosting and the other half with white frosting.

Yields two dozen cookies

BREAKFAST AT TIFFANY'S

TRUMAN CAPOTE

WE ATE LUNCH at the cafeteria in the park. Afterwards, avoiding the zoo (Holly said she couldn't bear to see anything in a cage), we giggled, ran, sang along the paths toward the old wooden boathouse, now gone. Leaves floated on the lake; on the shore, a park-man was fanning a bonfire of them, and the smoke, rising like Indian signals, was the only smudge on the quivering air. Aprils have never meant much to me, autumns seem that season of beginning, spring; which is how I felt sitting with Holly on the railings of the boathouse porch.

THE 59TH STREET BRIDGE SONG (FEELIN' GROOVY)

Paul Simon

Slow down, you move too fast.
You got to make the morning last.
Just kick-in' down the cobble stones,
Look-in' for fun and feel-in' groovy.

Hello lamppost,
What-cha know-in'
I've come to watch your flowers grow-in'
Ain't-cha got no rhymes for me?

Doot-in' doo-doo,
Feel-in' groovy.

Got no deeds to do,
No promises to keep.
I'm dappled and drowsy and ready to sleep.
Let the morning time drop all its petals on me.
Life, I love you, All is groovy.

N.Y. SONGS

How many songs celebrate the greatness, the suffering, the insanity, and the experience of being a New Yorker? We found 1,437. Luckily for you, we have honed the list down to the best of the best in classics, pop, rock, and jazz. From "Puttin' on the Ritz" and "Give My Regards to Broadway" to "Big Yellow Taxi" and "Scenes from and Italian Restaurant" these songs capture the essence of the city, what it means to be in New York, live in New York, and understand New York. Whether you are a seasoned city dweller or an occasional visitor, these songs will remind you of your favorite things about New York City.

Arthur's Theme (Best That You Can Do),
Peter W. Allen/Burt Bacharach

NYC, *Peter M. Amato/Desmond Child*

I Can't See New York, *Tori Amos*

Broadway Melody 1974,
Anthony G. Banks/Phil Collins/ Peter Gabriel/Stephen R. Hackett/Michael Rutherford

Be My Baby,
Jeff Barry/Ellie Greenwich/Phil Spector

Just Over the Brooklyn Bridge,
Alan Bergman/Marilyn Bergman/ Marvin Hamlisch

Manhattan After Dark,
Milton Berle/Jerry Seelen

Puttin' on the Ritz, *Irving Berlin*

New York 24/7, *Charlie Bisharat*

Summer in the City, *Steve Boone/John Sebastian/Mark Sebastian*

Aladdin Sane, *David Bowie*

Manhattan Lullaby,
Johnny Brandon/Bob Richardson

New York 1950's and 1960's,
Rudy Calzado/Larry Harlow/Tito Puente

Manhattan Rag, *Hoagy Carmichael*

Down and Out in New York City,
Ward L. Chandler/Barry De Vorzon

Broadway Ladies, *Ray Charles*

New York City Blues,
Philip Cody/Neil Sedaka

Give My Regards to Broadway,
George M. Cohan

Brooklyn Bridge, *Larry Cohn*

New York, *Paul Thomas Cook/Stephen Jones/*
Glen Matlock/Johnny Rotten

New York Girl, *Miles Davis*

42nd Street, *Al Dubin/Harry Warren*

Autumn in New York, *Vernon Duke*

Broadway Is My Street, *Jimmy Durante*

Talkin' New York, *Bob Dylan*

New York New York, *Fred Ebb/John Kander*

New York City Blues, *Duke Ellington*

YMCA, *Alan Ett/Scott G. Liggett*

(I Like New York in June)
How About You, *Ralph Freed/Burton Lane*

Broadway Rose,
Martin Fried/Otis Spencer/Eugene West

Heart in New York,
Benny Gallagher/Graham Lyle

Manhattan Downbeat,
Ira Gershwin/Harry Warren

Up on the Roof, *Gerry Goffin/Carole King*

Manhattan, *Herbie Hancock/Jean C. Hancock*

Manhattan, *Lorenz Hart/Richard Rodgers*

Manhattan Skyline,
Skitch Henderson/Frank Sinatra

New York Minute, *Don Henley/Dan*
Kortchmar/Jai L. Winding

Honky Tonk Women,
Mick Jagger/Keith Richards

Big Man on Mulberry Street, *Billy Joel*

Miami 2017 (Seen the Lights
Go Out on Broadway), *Billy Joel*

Movin' Out (Anthony's Song), *Billy Joel*

New York State of Mind, *Billy Joel*

Scenes From an Italian Restaurant,
Billy Joel

Mona Lisas and Mad Hatters,
Elton John/Bernie Taupin

Manhattan Beat, *Quincy Jones*

There's a Broken Heart For Every Light on Broadway, *Jack Keller/Larry Kolber*

New York City, *John Lennon*

Que Pasa New York, *John Lennon/Yoko Ono*

Frank Mills (from the musical Hair,) *Galt MacDermot/James Rado/ Gerome Ragni*

New York City Rhythm, *Barry Manilow/Martin Panzer*

Broadway Fools, *Branford Marsalis*

Freedom, *Paul McCartney*

New York City Rap, *Bobby McFerrin*

Big Yellow Taxi, *Joni Mitchell*

Chelsea Morning, *Joni Mitchell*

Scrapple from the Apple, *Charlie Parker*

New York (Dolls), *Darren Pasdernick*

I Happen to Like New York, *Cole Porter*

NYC Man, *Lou Reed*

Do Like You Do in New York, *William "Boz" Scaggs*

Manhattan, *Bob Seger*

The Boxer, *Paul Simon*

59th Street Bridge Song (Feelin' Groovy), *Paul Simon*

The Only Living Boy in New York, *Paul Simon*

The Poem on the Underground Wall, *Paul Simon*

The Sound of Silence, *Paul Simon*

Broadway Baby, *Stephen Sondheim*

New York City Serenade, *Bruce Springsteen*

Englishman in New York, *Sting*

Take the A-Train, *Billy Strayhorn*

Manhattan Melody, *Harry Warren*

Living For the City, *Stevie Wonder*

Part of the oncoming demise (of New York during its terrible fiscal crisis) is that none of us can simply believe it. We were always the best and the strongest of cities, and our people were vital to the teeth. Knock them down eight times and they would get up with that look in the eye which suggests the fight has barely begun.

—NORMAN MAILER

HARLEM

Langston Hughes

What happens to a dream deferred?

Does it dry up
like a raisin in the sun?
Or fester like a sore—
And then run?
Does it stink like rotten meat?
Or crust and sugar over—
like a syrupy sweet?

Maybe it just sags
like a heavy load.

Or does it explode?

JAZZ

TONI MORRISON

I'M CRAZY ABOUT THIS CITY.

Daylight slants like a razor cutting the buildings in half. In the top half I see looking faces and it's not easy to tell which are people, which the work of stonemasons. Below is shadow where any blasé thing takes place: clarinets and lovemaking, fists and the voices of sorrowful women. A city like this one makes me dream tall and feel in on things. Hep. It's the bright steel rocking above the shade below that does it. When I look over strips of green grass lining the river, at church steeples and into the cream-and-copper halls of apartment buildings, I'm strong. Alone, yes, but top-notch and indestructible—like the City in 1926 when all the wars are over and there will never be another one. The people down there in the shadow are happy about that. At last, at last, everything's ahead. The smart ones say so and people listening to them and reading what they write down agree: Here comes the new. Look out. There goes the sad stuff. The bad stuff. The things-nobody-could-help stuff. The way everybody was then and there. Forget that. History is over, you all, and everything's ahead at last.

TAKE THE 'A' TRAIN

Billy Strayhorn

You must Take The "A" Train
To go to Sugar Hill 'way up in Harlem.
If you miss the "A" train,
You'll find you've missed the quickest
   way to Harlem
Hurry, get on now it's coming
Listen to those rails a-thrumming
All 'board! get on The "A" Train
Soon you will be on Sugar Hill in
   Harlem.

189

$\mathcal{M}$elting pot Harlem—Harlem of honey and chocolate and caramel and rum and vinegar and lemon and lime and gall. Dusky dream Harlem rumbling into a nightmare tunnel where the subway from the Bronx keeps right on downtown.

—LANGSTON HUGHES

123RD STREET RAP

Willie Perdomo

A day on
123rd Street

goes a little
something like
this:

Automatic bullets
    bounce
off stoop steps

It's about time to pay
all my debts

Church bells bong for
drunken mourners

Baby men growing on
all the corners

Money that
ain't mine

Sun that
don't shine

Trees that
don't grow

Wind that
won't blow

Drug posses
ready to rumble

Ceilings starting
to crumble

Abuelas close
eyes and pray

While they watch
the children play

Not much I
can say

Except day turns
to night

And I can't tell what's
wrong from what's right

on 123rd Street

ATHEIST HIT BY TRUCK

JOHN McNULTY

THIS DRUNK came down the "L" stairs, and at the bottom he made a wrong turn. This led him into the gutter instead of onto the sidewalk, and a truck hit him and knocked him down.

It is a busy corner there at Forty-second Street and Second Avenue, in front of the Shanty, and there's a hack line there. Naturally, a little crowd and a cop gathered around the drunk and some hackies were in the crowd.

The cop was fairly young. After he hauled the guy up and sat him on the bottom step of the "L" stairs, he saw there wasn't much wrong with him. His pants were torn and maybe his knee was twisted slightly—maybe cut.

The cop got out his notebook and began asking questions and writing the answers down. Between questions he had to prop the man up. Fellow gave his name—Wilson, Martin, some noncommittal name—and his address. Everybody around was interested in these facts.

The blind man in the newspaper hut under the stairs felt a little put out because nobody was telling him what was going on, and he could hear beguiling fragments of it. "What happen? What

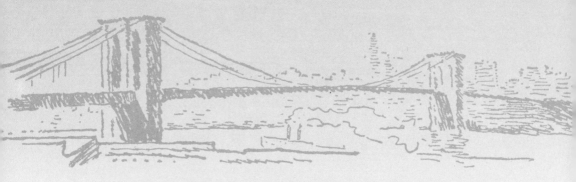

happen?" the blind man kept asking, but the event wasn't deemed sensational enough for anybody to run and tell him, at least until afterward.

"What religion are yuh?" the policeman asked the man, who propped himself up this time and blurted out, "Atheist! I'm an atheist!"

For some reason, a lot people laughed.

"Jeez, he's an atheist!" one of the hackies said. He shouted to a comrade who was still sitting behind the wheel of a parked cab at the corner, "Feller says he's an atheist!"

"Wuddaya laughing at?" the cop asked, addressing himself to the crowd generally. "Says he's an atheist, so he's an atheist. Wuddaya laughing at?" He wrote something in the book.

Another policeman, from over by Whelan's drugstore, where there was a picket line, strolled up. He was an older cop, more lines in his face, bigger belly, less humps around his hips, because the equipment—twisters, mace, and all that stuff—fitted on him better after all these years. "Wuzzamadder with 'im?" he asked his colleague.

"This here truck hit him. He isn't hurt bad. Says he's an atheist."

"I *am* an atheist!" the man yelled.

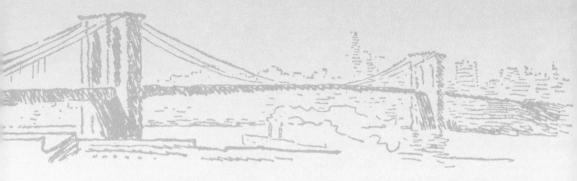

The crowd laughed again.

"Did you put that down—atheist?" the older cop asked.

"Yuh, I put it in where it says, 'religion.'"

"Rubbid out. Rubbid out. Put in Cat'lic. He looks like a Cat'lic to me. He got an Irish name? Anyway, rubbid out. When he sobers up, he'll be sorry he said that atheist business. Put in Cat'lic. We gotta send him to Bellevue just for safety's sake." The young cop started for the drugstore to put in a call.

"Never mind safety's sake. I'm an atheist, I'm telling you," the drunk said, loud as he could.

"Cuddid out, cuddid out," the older cop said. Then he leaned over like a lecturer or somebody. "An' another thing—if you wouldn't go round sayin' you're an atheist, maybe you wouldn't be gettin' hit by trucks."

The crowd sensed a great moral lesson and didn't laugh.

"Jeez! The guy says he's an atheist," the hackie said again.

A little later the Bellevue ambulance came.

"I yam a natheist," the man kept muttering as they put him into the ambulance.

A chowder is generally any thick soup, but the word usually refers to a mixture of fish and vegetables in either a cream or tomato base. "Chowder" is derived from the Latin word "calderia," which means "a place for warming things" or "cooking pot." In French "calderia" became "chaudiere" or "chaudron." Clam chowder became popular in New England and Canadian fishing villages in the 1700s. Manhattan clam chowder is made with tomatoes instead of cream, as in New England clam chowder. Many people claim that they created this recipe, but there is written documentation at the South Street Seaport Museum—the grandson of a fish vendor who catered political fundraisers wrote a letter telling his children that his grandfather invented the tomato-based version of the popular chowder.

MANHATTAN CLAM CHOWDER

3 slices bacon

1 large onion, chopped

2 garlic cloves, diced

2 celery stalks, chopped

2 medium-sized carrots, chopped

5–6 medium-sized potatoes (about 2 pounds), peeled and diced

2 cans (14 1/2 ounces each) diced tomatoes (do not drain)

1 cup chicken broth

1 bottle (8 ounces) clam juice

2 teaspoon fresh thyme

1 bay leaf

24–30 fresh littleneck clams, well cleaned and scrubbed

Salt and pepper to taste

1. Heat a 6-quart soup pot over medium-high heat. Add bacon and cook until crisp. Remove from pot and dice. Set aside.

2. Pour all but 2 tablespoons of rendered bacon fat from pot.

3. Add the onion, garlic, celery, and carrots and sauté for 6 to 8 minutes, or until tender, stirring frequently.

4. Add the remaining ingredients, except clams, and bring to a boil. Reduce the heat to low. Cover and simmer for 20 to 25 minutes, or until the potatoes are tender.

5. Raise heat to medium-high. Add clams and reserved bacon. Cook 4-7 minutes longer, or until the clams have opened, discarding any that do not.

6. Season with salt and pepper to taste and serve.

Serves four.

FOOD FACTS

The Bloody Mary was first served at the King Cole Bar in the St. Regis Hotel by Parisian bartender Ferdinand "Pete" Petriot.

Pasta Primavera, made with fettuccini noodles and vegetables, was created by Sirio Maccioni, owner of Le Cirque.

In 1964 in Buffalo, Terressa Bellisimo made an impromptu snack at her family's bar, the Anchor Bar. She deep fried some leftover chicken, added some hot sauce, and *voila*, the buffalo wing was born.

The potato chip was born in 1853 at the posh Moon's Lake House in Saratoga Springs when a customer complained that his fried potato was too thick. The ornery cook retorted by frying paper-thin potato slices. People loved them and the "Saratoga Chip" became a popular item all over the East Coast.

In 1877 the Hell Gate Brewery, established by German immigrant George Ehret, was the largest in the U.S. By 1879 there were 78 breweries in Manhattan and 43 in Brooklyn.

"Pie a la mode" was coined in the 1890s at the Cambridge Hotel in Cambridge, New York when a patron noted Professor Charles Watson Townsend, eating his apple pie with ice cream, was eating "pie *a la mode*" (meaning hip, or fashionable). When Townsend visited Delmonico's in New York City and ordered his regular dessert, the manager immediately added it to the menu. A reporter from *The New York Sun* overheard the exchange and wrote about the new dessert the next day.

During the 19th century, seafood was so abundant that lobsters were an everyday item, oysters were common at large fish houses, and caviar from the Hudson was served free in saloons.

Chocolate fondue was first served in 1956 at the Chalet Suisse by Konrad Egli.

The produce market at Hunts Point in the Bronx is the largest in the world, selling more than $100 million worth of produce each year.

The English muffin was created by Samuel Bath Thomas sometime around 1880 at his bakery on 20th Street.

Japanese-inspired *negimaki*, which is beef rolls and scallions with soy sauce, was first eaten at the New York restaurant Nippon in 1959.

Yogurt became popular when Daniel Carasso and Juan Metzger began producing it under the name "Dannon" at a small factory in the Bronx.

The Belgian waffle made its debut at the 1964 World's Fair in New York.

Sangria was invented at the New York World's Fair of 1964–65.

NEW YORK DRINKS

EGG CREAM

2 tablespoons chocolate syrup

6 ounces whole milk, chilled

6 ounces soda water, chilled

An egg cream is a New York specialty that has been around since the 1930s. Contrary to what the name suggests, there is no egg in an egg cream. When made properly it has a foamy froth on top that resembles beaten egg whites or the foam from a cappuccino.

1. Mix syrup and milk in a large glass. Add soda water slowly. Then, using a long spoon, stir quickly to create a head of foam.

2. Serve immediately with a straw.

Serves one.

MANHATTAN

1 3/4 ounces whiskey

1/4 ounce sweet vermouth

To celebrate the election of Governor Samuel Tilden, a bartender at the Manhattan Club invented the "Manhattan."

1. Combine whiskey and vermouth in a large glass over ice, pouring the vermouth first (since you only need a drop, by adding it first, you can pour out any excess).

2. Strain into a chilled stemmed martini glass. Garnish with a maraschino cherry.

Serves one.

LONG ISLAND ICED TEA

The Long Island Iced Tea recipe was first made at the Oak Beach Inn in Hampton Bays by a bartender named Rosebud (Robert Butt), sometime in the 1970s.

½ ounce vodka
½ ounce gin
½ ounce tequila
½ ounce Triple Sec
½ ounce light rum
1 ½ ounce sweet and sour mix
Splash of cola (for color)

1. Fill a large glass with ice. Combine all the liquor in the glass, followed by the sweet and sour and cola.

2. Garnish with a lemon wedge and serve.

Serves one.

MILKSHAKE

6–8 scoops of vanilla ice cream

2 cups milk

½ cup vanilla syrup

1 teaspoon vanilla extract

Milkshakes are an American original consisting of milk, ice cream, and flavored syrup or fruit. The drink is mixed in a blender and sometimes an egg is added to make it richer. In the old days of soda fountains, here's how you could order your shake: "Burn One All the Way"— a chocolate malted with chocolate ice cream; "Twist It, Choke It, and Make It Cackle"— a chocolate malted with an egg; "Shake One in the Hay"— strawberry shake; and a "White Cow"— vanilla shake. A milkshake is perfect with a burger and fries, or sipped by itself, but it's extra fun to use two straws and share with a pal.

1. Pour all ingredients into a blender and blend until smooth. The longer you blend the shake, the thinner it will become, so blend to your desired consistency.

2. Pour into two large glasses and serve. If desired, top with whipped cream and a maraschino cherry. Serve immediately with a straw.

Serves two.

VARIATIONS:

If you prefer, before blending you can add chocolate syrup for a chocolate shake, a heaping scoop of malted milk powder for a vanilla malt or, both for a chocolate malt.

FAMOUS SITES FROM AROUND THE STATE AND WHAT HAPPENED WHERE

George Washington was inaugurated the country's first president at New York's Federal Hall.

The first New York State snow sculpting competition was held in Watertown, New York in 1985.

Brooklyn novelty shop owners Morris and Rose Michtom made the first Teddy bear at the turn of last century, after seeing a cartoon of President Roosevelt sparing a cub on a hunting trip, and displayed it in their window.

The statue of King George III in Bowling Green was destroyed by riots in 1776, melted down, and turned into musket balls used to fire against the British during the Revolutionary War.

The original location for 1969's Woodstock Festival was Wallkill, NY, but the citizens of that town wouldn't let the festival take place. It moved to Max Yasgur's dairy farm in Sullivan County (50 miles from the town of Woodstock). More than 400,000 people attended the concert.

West Point is the oldest continuously-occupied military post in America. Washington transferred his headquarters there in 1779. Fortress West Point was never captured by the British, despite Benedict Arnold's treason. President Thomas Jefferson signed legislation establishing the U.S. Military Academy there in 1802.

In 1898 several baking companies merged to form the National Biscuit Company, Nabisco, and opened an industrial bakery on 9th Avenue between 15th and 16th Streets. By 1902, the company had its first nationwide success with Barnum's Animal Crackers, and, in 1912, sold its first Oreo Cookies. 15th Street at 9th Avenue is now named Oreo Way.

On June 28, 1969 a pre-dawn riot broke out when cops raided the Stonewall Inn, a gay bar on Christopher Street. The clash became the touchstone for the Gay Rights movement.

Ellis Island Immigration Station officially opened its doors on January 1, 1892. Annie Moore, a 15-year-old Irish girl, was the first arrival on line.

New York City was briefly the U.S. capital from 1789 to 1790.

In 1954, the carcass of a 75 foot, 70-ton finback whale was displayed next to Nathan's Famous Hot Dogs in Coney Island to lure customers in for a snack. When a heat wave hit, the decomposing carcass forced the Health Department to issue a summons.

On July 9, 1776 the Declaration of Independence was read aloud to General Washington's troops in New York.

The family home of songwriter John Howard Payne in East Hampton, New York has become a museum named for his well-loved classic, "Home, Sweet, Home." The native New Yorker wrote the song in 1822.

HOME, SWEET, HOME

John Howard Payne

'Mid pleasures and palaces though we may roam,
Be it ever so humble there's no place like home!
A charm from the skies seems to hallow us there,
Which, seek through the world, is ne'er met with elsewhere.

Home! Home! Sweet, sweet home!
There's no place like home!
There's no place like home!

An exile from home splendor dazzles in vain;
Oh, give me my lowly thatch'd cottage again!
The birds singing gaily that came at my call;
Give me them with the peace of mind dearer than all.
(Chorus)

I miss New York and its fairy-like towers
With Liberty's torch high in the air
I'd give all of California's damn flowers
For the sight of Washington Square.

—JESSIE TARBOX BEALS

THE DEATH AND LIFE OF GREAT AMERICAN CITIES

JANE JACOBS

THE STRETCH OF HUDSON STREET where I live is each day the scene of an intricate sidewalk ballet. I make my own first entrance into it a little after eight when I put out the garbage can, surely a prosaic occupation, but I enjoy my part, my little clang, as the droves of junior high school students walk by the center of the stage dropping candy wrappers. (How do they eat so much candy so early in the morning?)

While I sweep up the wrappers I watch the other rituals of morning: Mr. Halpert unlocking the laundry's handcart from its mooring to a cellar door, Joe Cornacchia's son-in-law stacking out the empty crates from the delicatessen, the barber bringing out his sidewalk folding chair, Mr. Goldstein arranging the coils of wire which proclaim the hardware store is open, the wife of the tenement's superintendent depositing her chunky three-year-old with a toy mandolin on the stoop, the vantage point from which he is learning the English his

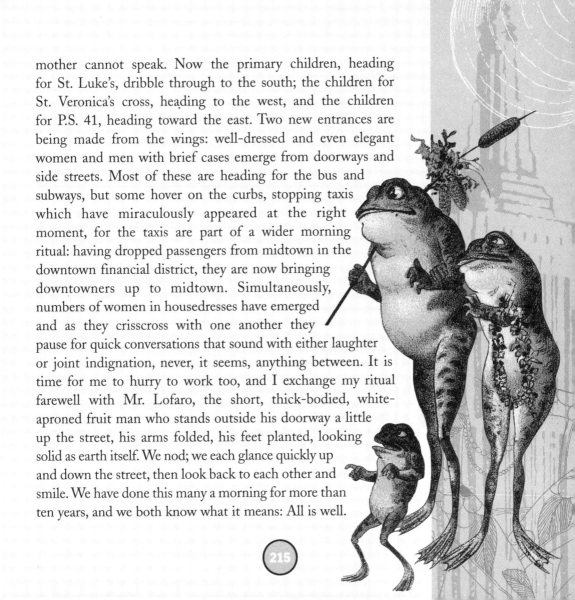

mother cannot speak. Now the primary children, heading for St. Luke's, dribble through to the south; the children for St. Veronica's cross, heading to the west, and the children for P.S. 41, heading toward the east. Two new entrances are being made from the wings: well-dressed and even elegant women and men with brief cases emerge from doorways and side streets. Most of these are heading for the bus and subways, but some hover on the curbs, stopping taxis which have miraculously appeared at the right moment, for the taxis are part of a wider morning ritual: having dropped passengers from midtown in the downtown financial district, they are now bringing downtowners up to midtown. Simultaneously, numbers of women in housedresses have emerged and as they crisscross with one another they pause for quick conversations that sound with either laughter or joint indignation, never, it seems, anything between. It is time for me to hurry to work too, and I exchange my ritual farewell with Mr. Lofaro, the short, thick-bodied, white-aproned fruit man who stands outside his doorway a little up the street, his arms folded, his feet planted, looking solid as earth itself. We nod; we each glance quickly up and down the street, then look back to each other and smile. We have done this many a morning for more than ten years, and we both know what it means: All is well.

215

MATZO BALL SOUP

*M*atzo ball soup is a staple during Passover (called Pesach in Hebrew) and consists of matzo balls (knaidel in Hebrew)—round dumplings made of matzo meal, eggs, and shortening (traditionally chicken fat)—in a chicken broth. Matzo is an unleavened bread that is a symbolic food for Jews. When the Jews were leaving Egypt, there was no time to wait for the bread to rise, and what they were left with was matzo. Matzo ball soup is sometimes called known as "Jewish Penicillin" because chicken broth has been proven to have beneficial medicinal properties. It's also a delightful comfort food. Since 1998, Ben's Kosher Deli in New York City has held a Matzo Ball Eating Championship, during which contestants must eat as many matzo balls as possible in five minutes and 25 seconds.

MATZO BALL SOUP

MATZO BALL SOUP

1 whole chicken
(3–4 pounds), washed
and patted dry, giblets
removed and discarded

Kosher salt and
pepper to taste

Chicken Broth

2 leeks,
cleaned thoroughly
and chopped

1 stalk celery,
including leaves, chopped

4 large carrots,
chopped into
1-inch pieces

2 large onions, quartered

4 whole garlic cloves

12 whole peppercorns,
crushed

1 bunch parsley,
preferably Italian,
finely chopped

$1/2$ teaspoon dried thyme

$1/2$ teaspoon dried dill

1. Salt the entire chicken, inside and out, with kosher or coarse salt and let stand for 30 minutes.

2. Wash salt from chicken and place in a large stockpot along with all the other ingredients except the parsley. Cover with cold water.

3. Bring to a boil over high heat. When at a rolling boil, reduce heat to simmer and cook for 1 to 1 $1/2$ hours, occasionally skimming any foam that collects at the top.

4. Remove chicken from pot and shred the meat once cool enough to handle.

5. Salt and pepper stock to taste. Don't be skittish with the seasoning. It may seem like a lot, but remember, you're flavoring several quarts of liquid. Add chopped parsley.

6. Keep stock and vegetables warm while you make your matzo balls.

Serves 4 to 6.

MATZO BALL SOUP

MATZO BALLS

4 large eggs

$^1/_2$ cup club soda

3 tablespoons
vegetable oil
or chicken fat (schmaltz)

Salt and pepper to taste

2 tablespoons parsley,
preferably Italian,
finely chopped

1 cup matzo meal

1. In a medium bowl, whisk eggs until blended. Add the club soda, oil (or schmaltz), salt, and pepper. Blend in the parsley and matzo meal.

2. Cover and refrigerate for about 1 hour. Bring a large pot of salted water to a boil.

3. Lightly grease your hands with vegetable oil and form balls from the refrigerated matzo mixture. You should use about two tablespoons per ball (Note: they plump as you cook 'em).

4. Drop matzo balls into boiling water. Reduce heat to medium-low and simmer for 25 to 30 minutes.

5. To Serve: In each bowl, place 2–3 matzo balls, some reserved shredded chicken, vegetables from the stock pot, and enough broth to cover. Serve and enjoy.

Yields 12 to 15 Matzo balls.

NEW YORK JEW

ALFRED KAZIN

THE NEXT MORNING I went as usual to my office. It was a brilliantly clear day, and usually it was impossible in that office, overlooking the heaped-up splendor of New York, to feel oneself less than brilliant. It was from working in that building that I knew why every sentence in *Time* had to strike like a rapier, shine like steel. The rows of metal desks glistened in the light. Brilliantly resourceful girls—researchers, who were not allowed to write— walked back and forth on editorial errands to their writers. Early as it was, one writer a cubicle away from me could already be heard chanting to himself from the Bhagavad-Gita. Another was sending out to the hall on his portable phonograph the allegretto from Beethoven's Seventh. The old boys were coming in from Ossining and Greenwich and Stamford with their impressively scuffed English attaché cases, saying witty doomsday things to each other, like characters in a John Cheever story, about the daily disasters of country living. Down in the concourse, where the city mob flowing out into the Fiftieth Street station of the Independent met the tourists with circular tickets around their necks looking with awe at every last wonder in Rockefeller Center, the chromium and steel frames around the window glass glistened more brightly than ever while on the wings of light itself messages sped from the cable center to every corner of the world. And I was part of it all....

I WANT NEW YORK

OGDEN NASH

I think those people are utterly unreliable
Who say they'd be happy on a desert island with a copy of the Biable
And Hamlet (by Shakespeare) and Don Quixote (by Cervantes)
And poems by Homer and Virgil and perhaps a thing or two of Dante's
And furthermore, I have a feeling that if they were marooned till the
     millennium's dawn
Very few of us would notice that they were gone.
Perhaps they don't like my opinions any better than I like theirs,
But who cares?
If I were going to be marooned and could take only one thing along
I'd be perfectly happy if I could take the thing which is the subject of
     this song.
I don't mean anything that was brought either by the postman or the
     stork.
I mean the City of New York.
For New York is a wonder city, a veritable fairyland
With many sights not to be seen in Massachusetts or Maryland.
It is situated on the island of Manhattan
Which I prefer to such islands as Welfare or Staten.
And it is far superior
To the cities of the interior.

What if it has a heterogeneous populace?

That is one of the privileges of being a metropulace

And heterogeneous people don't go around bothering each other

And you can be reasonably sure that everything you do won't get right back
to your dear old mother.

In New York beautiful girls can become more beautiful by going to
Elizabeth Arden

And getting stuff put on their faces and waiting for it to harden

And poor girls with nothing to their names but a letter or two can get rich
and joyous

From a brief trip to their loyous.

And anybody with a relative of whose will he is the beneficiary

Can do pretty well in the judiciary.

So I can say with impunity

That New York is a city of opportunity.

It also has many fine theaters and hotels,

And a lot of taxis, buses, subways and els,

Best of all, if you don't show up at the office or at a tea nobody will bother
their head

They will just think you are dead.

That's why I really think New York is exquisite.

It isn't all right just for a visit

But by God's Grace

I'd live in it and like it even better if you gave me the place.

THE MOB

In 1954, Bronx-born John Gotti was injured when, in the process of stealing a cement mixer from a construction site, the mixer tipped over, crushing his toes.

Gotti, *aka* "Dapper Don" became the head of the Gambino crime family in 1985. He was finally indicted in 1991 on racketeering and murder conspiracy charges.

Charles "Lucky" Luciano first met Meyer Lansky at P.S. 19 on 14th street. Lucky bullied kids for pennies, but Meyer fought back and they became lifelong friends.

The Rain-bo-room at the former Kenmore Hotel in Albany was a favorite haunt for notorious gangster Legs Diamond. He was reportedly shot and killed there.

Lucky Luciano was imprisoned in 1936 for running a prostitution ring, but was released in 1942 when the government asked for his help securing New York harbor after the explosion of the *Normandie*.

From 1933–1936, Luciano lived at the Waldorf-Astoria Towers, in suite 39D, under the alias Charles Ross.

※

La Cosa Nostra means "this thing of ours." Also known as the Mafia, the mob, the outfit, the office, it is a collection of Italian-American organized crime "families" operating in America since the 1920s.

※

The Bonanno, the Colombo, the Genovese (the largest), the Gambino, and the Lucchese families make up *La Cosa Nostra* in New York City.

※

"Murder Incorporated" was a group of Sicilian and Jewish criminals in the 1930s that carried out up to 1000 contract killings. They included Luciano, Lansky, Joe Adonis, Frank Costello, Louis "Lepke" Buchalter, and Albert Anastasia.

※

Mobster Owney Madden started The Cotton Club in 1923. The house band was led by Duke Ellington and the line-up included Cab Calloway, Louis Armstrong, and Lena Horne.

※

The Government estimated that between 1979 and 1984, the Mafia imported $1.6 billion dollars worth of heroin.

※

Arnold Rothstein, *aka* A.R. *aka* Mr. Big, *aka* The Fixer, *aka* The Big Bankroll, *aka* The Man Uptown, *aka* The Brain inspired the characters of Meyer Wolfsheim in *The Great Gatsby* and Nathan Detroit in *Guys and Dolls*. He was rumored to be behind the fixing of the 1919 World Series.

※

The five families at times have controlled the Fulton Fish Market, the Javits Convention Center, the New York Coliseum, and air cargo operations at JFK Airport.

DEBAUCHERY, SQUALOR, VICE, AND VIOLENCE epitomized Five Points, the 19th century neighborhood that was the basis for Martin Scorsese's epic film *Gangs of New York*. Named for the intersection of Mulberry, Anthony (now Worth), Cross (now Mosco), Orange (now Baxter), and Little Water (no longer there) Streets, this small area encompassed America's most wretched poverty. Five Points was the scene of more riots, corruption, saloons, and brothels than any other neighborhood in the New World.

Five Points was built over the once bucolic Collect Pond. Pollution from nearby slaughterhouses and tanneries contaminated the water, so it was filled in as a public works project in the early 1800s. By 1813, frame houses were constructed and occupied by middle-class people and tradesmen, who combined their homes and businesses. In the 1820s, the Collect Pond landfill decayed and the houses began to sag and sink. The area became foul smelling and infested with mosquitoes and disease, and most respectable residents moved out. Only the destitute remained, becoming victims of slumlords, gangs, and ruthless politicians looking for votes. With the huge influx of immigrants, greedy landlords divided the decrepit houses into even smaller living quarters, with no regard for safety or sanitation. The filthy conditions and lack of clean water led to an outbreak of cholera in New York City in 1832, with one third of all cases from the Five Points area.

When all the houses were filled, shabbily constructed tenements designed to house as many people as possible were hastily built. Coulter's Brewery, which brewed beer until the mid-1830s, was converted into the rowdiest and most dangerous apartment house in the area, known as the Old Brewery. It contained the "Den of Thieves," a single room that housed about 75 men and women and became overrun with criminals and prostitutes.

Early on, the population of Five Points was largely African-American—freed slaves who couldn't afford to live anywhere else. The subsequent massive immigration of Irish and Germans made Five Points the most densely packed neighborhood in all of New York, and by 1855 the Irish population had reached nearly 10,000, second in size only to Dublin. Day-to-day survival often required that all members of the family bring in money, by whatever means possible.

By the 1850s, Five Points was ruled by gangs, including the Plug Uglies, the Roach Guards, and the Dead Rabbits. Several Five Pointers became prominent mob figures years later during Prohibition, including Al Capone and Lucky Luciano. The neighborhood also became notorious for electoral lawlessness, with Five Points' precincts casting as many as two or three times more ballots than there were eligible voters.

Charity groups attempted to clean up the area in the 1850s, establishing the Five Points Mission in the site of the Old Brewery. By the end of the Civil War, the neighborhood had cleaned up a bit, but the next wave of Italian and Chinese immigrants replaced the Irish and African-Americans, once again creating a slum.

Danish reformer Jacob Riis brought attention to the wretched area in the 1880s, prompting a campaign to eliminate the neighborhood altogether. The city acquired and condemned most of the tenements between 1887 and 1894, and eventually built courthouses and state offices that still stand in Foley Square. Part of the Five Points area is now home to Chinatown. The wretched neighborhood that was once the most despondent and dangerous place in America is now a bustling and thriving community.

MANHATTAN

Lorenz Hart

Summer journeys to Niagara
And to other places aggravate all our
     cares;
We'll save our fares;
I've a cozy little flat in what is known as
     old Manhattan
We'll settle down right here in town:

We'll have Manhattan
The Bronx and Staten Island too;
It's lovely going through the Zoo;
It's very fancy
On old Delancey Street, you know;
The subway charms us so,
When balmy breezes blow
To and fro;
And tell me what street
compares with Mott Street in July,
Sweet pushcarts gently gliding by:

The great big city's a wond'rous toy
Just made for a girl and boy
We'll turn Manhattan
Into an isle of joy.

We'll go to Greenwich
Where modern men itch To be free;
And Bowling Green you'll see with me;
We'll bathe at Brighton
The fish you'll frighten
When you're in
Your bathing suit so thin
Will make the shellfish grin
Fin to fin;
I'd like to take a sail on Jamaica Bay
     with you;
And fair Canarsie's Lakes we'll view

The city's bustle cannot destroy
The dreams of a girl and boy
We'll turn Manhattan
Into an isle of joy.

We'll go to Yonkers
Where true love conquers In the wilds;

And starve together, dear, in Childs'
We'll go to Coney
And eat bologny on a roll;
In Central Park, we'll stroll
Where our first kiss we stole,
Soul to soul;
Our future babies we'll take to Abie's
    Irish Rose.
I hope they'll live to see it close.
The city's clamor can never spoil
The dreams of a boy and goil
We'll turn Manhattan
    Into an isle of joy.

We'll have Manhattan
The Bronx and Staten Island, too;
We'll try to cross Fifth Avenue;
As black as onyx We'll find the Bronnix
    Park Express;
Our Flatbush flat, I guess
Will be a great success.
More or less;
A short vacation on Inspiration Point
    we'll spend
And in the station house we'll end
But Civic Virtue cannot destroy
The dreams of a girl and boy
We'll turn Manhattan
    Into an isle of joy.

If you're eating a bagel that is perfectly round, with a symmetrical hole smack dab in the center, then you are not eating an authentic New York City bagel. Bagels are boiled and then baked to produce a crispy outer crust and a chewy inside, and never have a uniform shape. New York City bagels are said to be different (and better!) than all other bagels because the quality of New York City water creates a specific consistency unlike that produced in all other regions. The word "bagel" is thought to derive from the Yiddish "beygel," and the German "bügel," meaning a round loaf of bread. Some historians credit a Viennese baker who wanted to bake special bread to honor of King Jan III of Poland, a skilled horseman, for saving the city from Turkish invaders in 1683. The baker fashioned bread into the shape of a "buegel" or stirrup. The Community Regulations of Cracow for 1610 stated that "beygls" be given as a gift to women in childbirth. Some cultures regard the circular shape as the continuous life cycle and good luck. Cream cheese was marketed in the early 1900s and immediately became the preferred spread for a bagel. The first frozen bagel was sold in 1962. Whatever the history, whatever the topping, a bagel is the ultimate New York City breakfast food.

BAGELS

A New York bagel can't be beat. Here's one classic version of how they are often eaten.

NEW YORK, NEW YORK BAGEL

Bagel
Cream cheese
Lox
Sliced tomato
Capers
Sliced red onion
Cucumber (optional)

Slice and toast the bagel. Then top to your heart's delight with the ingredients at left. OR try some of these classic recipes:

WHITEFISH SALAD

2 pounds smoked whitefish*
2 stalks celery, diced
1 cup sour cream
1 1/2 tablespoons mayonnaise
1 tablespoon fresh dill, chopped, plus extra for garnish
1 tablespoon parsley, chopped, plus extra for garnish
Salt and pepper to taste
*Smoked whitefish is available at most supermarkets and even in some delis.

1. Remove the skin, head, and bones from the whitefish and place meat in a large bowl.

2. Add the remaining ingredients and fold together.

3. If you prefer a richer, creamier salad, feel free to use more sour cream and mayonnaise than listed above.

4. Garnish with additional sprigs of dill and parsley and serve.

Serves 4.

BAGELS

1 pound cream cheese
$^1/_2$ cup sour cream
1 teaspoon salt
1 teaspoon garlic powder
$^1/_2$ cup scallions, chopped

SCALLION CREAM CHEESE

In a large bowl combine all ingredients,
except scallions, and beat until smooth.
Stir in scallions and serve with toasted bagels.

Serves 8 to 10.

$^1/_4$ pound sliced smoked salmon
12 eggs
$^1/_2$ cup heavy cream
4 ounces cream cheese, diced
Salt and pepper to taste
2 tablespoons butter
12 to 15 blades of fresh chives,
finely chopped or snipped

SOFT-SCRAMBLED EGGS
WITH SMOKED SALMON AND CHIVES

1. Reserve 2 slices of salmon for garnish.

2. Chop the remaining salmon into very small
   pieces.

3. Whisk eggs and cream together.
   Add $^1/_2$ of chopped chives and
   season with salt and pepper.

4. Preheat a large nonstick skillet over medium
   heat. Melt the butter until it foams, then
   turn the heat down to low and slowly
   pour in the eggs and cream cheese. Slowly
   stir the eggs from the outside of the pan
   to the center. Once the eggs begin to set,
   stirring slowly will create large, cloud-like
   curds. Take care not to let the eggs brown,

BAGELS

and even if you get tempted, don't try and speed the process by turning up the heat (even if you think the eggs aren't cooking, they are). This process will take time, but in the end you will have eggs that are soft and custard-like. It will take about 10 minutes.

5. Scramble eggs gently and slowly. Do not cook the eggs until dry, you want them creamy. When they have come together but remain wet, stir in chopped salmon. Remove pan from the stove and place on a trivet. Garnish with remaining salmon and chives. Serve.

Yields 8 to 10.

VARIATION:
Leave out the salmon and add ¹/₂ cup chopped green onions. Sauté them lightly in the butter before adding the eggs and you have EGGS and ONIONS. Garnish with chopped tomato and serve.

BAGELS

Here are a few other ways to dress your bagel up if you want to take a vacation from the Big Apple:

BRUSCHETTA BAGEL:
Top a toasted bagel with a mixture of tomatoes, garlic, and basil.

CROQUE BAGEL:
Smoked ham, Swiss cheese, and mustard, under a broiler until the cheese is melted and bubbling.

CREPE BAGEL:
Nutella and banana on a chocolate chip or raisin bagel.

FALL BAGEL:
Bosc pears, blue cheese, and chopped pecans on a toasted bagel, drizzled with a little balsamic vinegar.

RISE-AND-SHINE BAGEL:
Fried egg, ketchup, and turkey bacon on a toasted poppy seed bagel.

BENEDICT BAGEL:
Poached egg, Canadian bacon, and hollandaise.

SOUTH OF THE BORDER BAGEL:
Jalapeño or cheese bagel topped with guacamole, refried beans, salsa, Monterey Jack cheese, and chorizo or chicken sausage.

NEBBISH BAGEL:
Chopped liver, chopped boiled egg, and salted butter on a rye bagel.

KING OF THE SEA:
Tuna salad, lettuce, cucumber, and mayo. Melted cheddar optional.

BAGELS

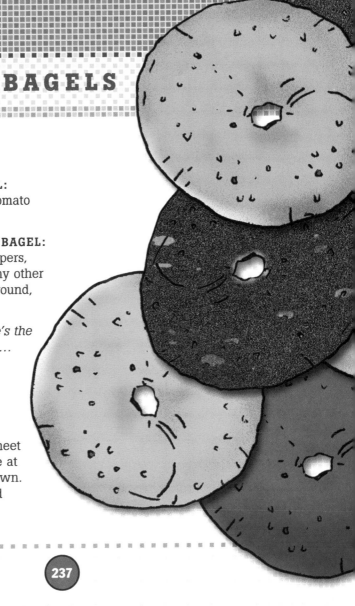

MIDDLE EASTERN BAGEL:
Hummus, tabouli, sliced tomato
on an everything bagel.

SAN FRANCISCO HAVEN BAGEL:
Avocado, tomato, bell peppers,
cucumber, sprouts, and any other
veggie you have laying around,
on a whole wheat bagel.

*And then, of course, there's the
great Bagel Resting Place...*

BAGEL CHIPS!
Slice your unused or
unwanted bagels
about $1/4$ inch thick.

Place them on a cookie sheet
in a single layer and bake at
350° F until crisp and brown.
Serve with dip or mustard
and pickles.

237

NEW YORK CITY: Land of brigands, where morals are loose, and one must be forever vigilant against threat of physical and/or spiritual corruption. Such has been an oft-voiced opinion of the metropolis. Whether true or false, it's not for lack of trying on the part of local and state legislators. In addition to legal prohibitions on all the societal no-nos one might expect, over the years many other unusual acts have run afoul of New York's lawmakers.

Here follows a sampling of some of the lesser-known, yet sensible restrictions, along with some other (more sublimely ridiculous) ones. Cole Porter may have written, "Anything Goes"—well, not in New York, buddy! (And these laws were written before smoking was banned...)

STATE LAWS

A fine of $25 can be levied for flirting. This old law specifically prohibits men from turning around on any city street and looking "at a woman in that way."

A second conviction for a crime of this magnitude calls for the violating male to be forced to wear a "pair of horse-blinders" wherever and whenever he goes outside for a stroll.

It is against the law to throw a ball at someone's head for fun.

A person may not walk around on Sundays with an ice cream cone in his/her pocket.

While riding in an elevator, one must talk to no one, and fold his hands while looking toward the door.

Slippers are not to be worn after 10:00 P.M.

It is against the law for a blind person to drive an automobile.

It is illegal to shoot a rabbit from a moving trolley car.

CITY LAWS

ALBANY
You cannot play golf in the streets.

BROOKLYN
Donkeys are not allowed to sleep in bathtubs.

CARMEL
A man can't go outside while wearing a jacket and pants that do not match.

GREENE
During a concert, it is illegal to eat peanuts and walk backwards on the sidewalks.

NEW YORK
It is illegal for a woman to be on the street wearing "body hugging clothing."

It is disorderly conduct for one man to greet another on the street by placing the end of his thumb against the tip of his nose and wiggling the extended fingers of that hand.

Women may go topless in public, providing it is not being used to advertise a business.

Since 1978, New York City dog owners have been required by law to clean up after their pets. It's estimated that before the law, approximately 40 million pounds of dog excrement piled up on the streets annually.

A New York City ordinance states that jumping from a building is punishable by death.

OCEAN CITY
It is illegal for men to go topless in the center of town.

SAG HARBOR
It is illegal to disrobe in a wagon.

If one wishes to bathe in the city limits, they must be clothed in a "suitable bathing suit."

STATEN ISLAND
You may only water your lawn if the hose is held in your hand.

WOODSTOCK
It is illegal to walk your bear on the street without a leash.

MODERN SPORTS

FRAN LEBOWITZ

WHEN IT COMES TO SPORTS I am not particularly interested. Generally speaking, I look upon them as dangerous and tiring activities performed by people with whom I share nothing except the right to trial by jury. It is not that I am totally indifferent to the joys of athletic effort—it is simply that my idea of what constitutes sport does not coincide with popularly held notions of the subject. There are a number of reasons for this, chief among them being that to me the outdoors is what you must pass through in order to get from your apartment into a taxicab.

There *are*, however, several contests in which I *do* engage and not, I might add, without a certain degree of competence. The following is by no means a complete list:

1. Ordering in Some Breakfast.
2. Picking Up the Mail.
3. Going Out for Cigarettes.
4. Meeting for a Drink.

As you can see, these are largely urban activities and, as such, not ordinarily regarded with much respect by sports enthusiasts. Nevertheless, they all require skill, stamina, and courage. And they all have their penalties and their rewards.

There are many such activities and I, for one, feel that the time is ripe for them to receive proper recognition. I therefore propose that those in charge of the 1980 Olympic Games invite New York to participate as a separate entity. The New York team would be entered in only one contest, to be called the New York Decathlon. The New York Decathlon would consist of four events instead of the usual ten, since everyone in New York is very busy. It would further differ from the conventional decathlon in that each contestant would enter only one event, since in New York it pays to specialize. The four events would be Press Agentry, Dry Cleaning and Laundering, Party-going, and Dog-owning.

Traditionally the Olympic Games open with a torch-bearer followed by all the athletes marching around the stadium carrying flags. This will not be changed, but in 1980 the athletes will be followed by seventeen Checker cabs carrying the New York team. The first cabby in line will have his arm out the window and in his hand will be a torch. The passengers in this cab will be screaming at the cabby as sparks fly into the back seat. He will pretend not to hear them. When the parade concludes, the first cabby will fail to notice this immediately and he will be compelled to stop short. This will cause all the following cabs to run into each other. The cabbies will then spend the rest of the Olympics yelling at each other and writing things down in a threatening manner. The athletics teams will be forced to start the games even though this collision has occurred where it will cause the greatest inconvenience.

PRESS AGENTRY

The two contestants enter the stadium from opposite sides, having first been assured by the referee that both sides are equally important. They kiss each other on both cheeks and turn smartly toward the crowd. They do not look past the first ten rows. They then seat themselves on facing Ultrasuede sofas and light cigarettes. Two moonlighting ball boys race in with coffee black, no sugar. The contestants pick up their ringing phones. Points awarded as follows:

243

1. For not taking the most calls from people who wish to speak to you.
2. For waking up the most people who do not.
3. For telling the most people who want to attend an event that they can't have tickets.
4. For telling the most people who do not want to attend said event that you have already sent them tickets by messenger and that they owe you a favor.

DRY CLEANING AND LAUNDERING

Two fully equipped dry cleaning and laundering establishments are constructed in inconvenient areas of the stadium. Several innocent people enter each establishment. These people serve the same function in this event that the fox serves in a hunt. They place upon the counter piles of soiled clothing, receive little slips of colored paper, and leave. Points awarded as follows:

1. For ripping off the most buttons.
   a. Additional points if buttons are impossible to replace.
2. For washing the most silk shirts bearing labels stating DRY CLEAN ONLY.

> a. Additional points if shirts are washed with bleeding madras jackets.
>
> b. If shirts are white, victory is near.

3. For boxing the most shirts requested on hangers.
4. For losing the most garments.
    > a. Additional points according to expensiveness of garments.
5. For being the most ingenious in moving ink spots from one pant leg to the other.

PARTY-GOING

A room exactly half the size necessary is built in the center of the stadium. Too many contestants enter the room. Points awarded as follows:

1. For getting to the bar.
2. For getting away from the bar.
3. For accidentally spilling wine on an opponent to whom you have lost a job.
4. For inadvertently dropping a hot cigarette ash on same.
5. For making the greatest number of funny remarks about people not present.

245

6. For arriving the latest with the greatest number of famous people.
7. For leaving the earliest with an old lover's new flame.

DOG-OWNING

There has been erected in the stadium an exact replica of a fifteen-block section of Greenwich Village. Twenty contestants leave buildings on the perimeter of this area, each walking three dogs who have not been out of the house all day. The object of the game is to be the first to get to the sidewalk directly in front of my building.

When all of the points are added up, the contestant with the greatest number of points enters the stadium. He is followed by the two contestants with the next greatest number of points. The two runners-up go off to one side with the referee. The referee takes out a stopwatch. Each runner-up has five minutes in which to explain in an entertaining manner why *he* did not receive the most points. Whichever runner-up is the more arrogant and convincing is presented with the gold medal. Because in New York it's not whether you win of lose—it's how you lay the blame.

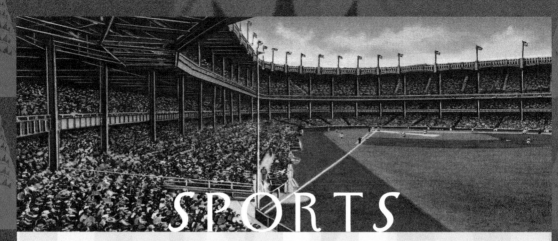

SPORTS

The Brooklyn Dodgers were once known as the Trolley Dodgers and the Brooklyn Bridegrooms.

In 1957, New Yorker Althea Gibson became the 1st black woman to win the world championship in tennis.

The first "Subway Series" predates the subway; in 1889 the National League champion New York Giants beat the American Association champion Brooklyn Bridegrooms 6-3. The first modern subway series was played in 1921, when the Giants beat the Yankees.

Babe Ruth hit his first home run in Yankee Stadium in the first game ever played there, in 1923.

The Brooklyn Dodgers won their only championship in Brooklyn in 1955.

The corporate name of the Mets is the "New York Metropolitan Baseball Club, Inc." On May 8, 1961 New York's National League club announces that the team nickname will be "Mets."

The country's oldest municipal golf course, opened in 1895, is in Van Cortlandt Park in the Bronx.

✥

September 24, 1957: say good riddance to "Dem Bums." The Brooklyn Dodgers play their last game at Ebbets Field—defeating the Pittsburgh Pirates 2-0.

✥

Many believe that Madison Square Park is the birthplace of baseball, since Alexander Cartwright formed the first baseball club—the New York Knickerbockers—there in 1845.

✥

The New York Knickerbockers, known as the Knicks, are one of only two charter members of the National Basketball Association still in their original cities.

✥

Originally called the Bisons, The Buffalo Bills football team got their name in 1946 after running a contest to select a new name. Over 4,500 entries were submitted, and "Bills" won over "Bullets," "Nickels," and "Blue Devils."

✥

Wade Boggs and Cal Ripken Jr. played against each other in Rochester vs. the Pawtucket Red Sox in 1981 in the longest game in baseball history. The game went a total of 33 innings.

✥

Saratoga Race Track is the oldest thoroughbred race track in the nation.

✥

Tennis was introduced to America by Mary Outerbridge, who oversaw the construction of the first lawn court at the Staten Island Cricket and Baseball Club.

✥

Jake LaMotta, a middleweight boxer known as the "Bronx Bull," was the subject of Scorcese's *Raging Bull*, starring New Yorker Robert DeNiro.

HOT DOGS

*T*he ultimate street food in NYC, perfect with sauerkraut and mustard, is related to the common European sausage brought to the U.S. by several ethnic groups. The term "hot dog" is thought to come from T.A. Dorgan, a sports cartoonist, who was watching a game at the Polo Grounds on a cold day in 1901. He drew a dachshund between two slices of bread and called it a "hot dog" because he couldn't spell dachshund. In 1871 Charles Feltman, a German butcher, opened up the first Coney Island hot dog stand and sold 3,684 dachshund (or "little-dog") sausages during his first year in business. Nathan Handwerker, a former employee of Feltman, opened Nathan's Famous Hot Dogs and competed with Feltman's by charging only five cents per dog, instead of ten cents. When people began questioning the quality of his cheaper dog, he offered free hot dogs to interns at Coney Island Hospital on the condition that

12 all-beef hot dogs

12 buns

Sauerkraut

Spicy mustard

Onion sauce
(recipe follows)

ONION SAUCE:
3 yellow onions,
peeled and sliced

3 cloves
garlic, minced

2 tablespoons
olive oil

$1/4$ cup marinara
sauce
(bottled is fine)

$1 1/2$ tablespoons
paprika

$1/4$ teaspoon
cayenne (optional)

Salt to taste

they come to his stand wearing their white coats. Nathan's gained a reputation for being the place where the doctors ate. Since 1916, Nathan's has hosted an annual hot dog eating contest on July 4th. These days, practically everyone in the United States eats hot dogs. Check out these stats:

In New York, there is only one true way to eat a hot dog. It can be butter-fried, grilled, pan-fried, or boiled. The bun can be toasted or not, seeded or regular. What's important is what goes on the dog, and this is the classic combination: mustard, sauerkraut, and onion sauce. Put the ketchup DOWN! It has no place here!

1. Sauté garlic and onions in olive oil. When onions are tender, add marinara sauce, cayenne, and paprika. Simmer over a low heat for about 15 minutes. Add salt to taste. Toss on your dog.

Serves 12.

MY CONEY ISLAND UNCLE

BY HARVEY SWADOS

I DIDN'T KNOW HOW to tell Uncle Dan that he was my favorite. The other New York uncles were all right, but they had wives and children of their own; he was the one who I felt belonged to me. People said that I looked like him, which was beyond my understanding—he was a burly man with an impudent mop of reddish-brown hair (my father had almost none that I can recall even from my earliest childhood, and I couldn't even tell you the color of the fringe around his ears), and an even more unlikely mustache, full, square, and bristling. How could I resemble a middle-aged man—he must have been in his thirties at that

time—with a big thick mustache? It was enough that he would give me a dog, and an occasional boot in the behind, to show me that he appreciated what I didn't dare to tell him....

I was going on thirteen that summer, sullen and rebellious after the circus fiasco, when my father informed me with clumsily evasive tact that, as a reward for having done well in school and helped out at the store, I was to be sent to New York. Alone.

If they had fixed it up not with my Coney Island uncle but with the Manhattan uncles, Al or Eddie, I probably wouldn't even have wanted to go at all. Not that I was spoiled or blasé about New York. But mother and I had always stayed with Uncle Al and Aunt Clara, mother sleeping on the studio couch, me bunking with their boys.

I just knew that it would be different now, staying with my Coney Island uncle. From the moment that father bade me goodbye in the unwashed bus depot that smelled of depression and defeat, stowing his rusty Gladstone in the rack over my head, shaking hands with me shyly, and smiling a reassurance that did not conceal his perpetual somberness, I settled into the new mood of freedom and

adventure. All through the long ride down across
Pennsylvania, Erie to Warren to Coudersport to Towanda
to Scranton to New York, I pitched and rolled on the torn
leather seat with the stuffing oozing out, exalted as though
I strode the deck of a Yankee clipper. Even the discovery
that my uncle was not at the Manhattan Greyhound
Terminal to meet me, as he had promised, was exhilarating.
I kept a good grip on the valise, as father had advocated,
and while I was looking about for Uncle Dan, a lady from
Travelers Aid came up and asked if I was Charley Morrison.

"Your uncle is tied up in an emergency. He says to
come right out to his place. Now you can take any line of
the BMT, can you remember that? Don't take the IRT, you'll
get all mixed up."

It was like Uncle Dan, I thought, not to send some
stooge relative after me, but to trust me, even though it
was already well into the night, to find my way out to
Coney Island. I got there without trouble, hauled the valise
down the steps of the elevated into the street at Surf
Avenue, and walked straight up the block, milling and
restless as Times Square, even at midnight, to the corner
where Uncle Dan's signs hung in all his second-floor

windows. Just as I was reaching out to punch his night bell I heard my uncle's familiar voice behind me, deep and drawling.

"Charley boy! Have a nice ride?"

I swung around. Uncle Dan was standing there smiling, medical bag in his left hand, cigar and door key in his right. His hat was shoved back on his head, and his Palm Beach suit was wrinkled at the crotch; he had put on some weight and seemed tired, but otherwise he looked the same.

"Let's just throw our bags in the hall, so we can go out and grab a bite."

He led me around the corner and up the ramp, gritty with sand, to the boardwalk. Above us the looped wires of bulbs drooped like heavy necklaces, the neon lights of stores and stands slashed on and off, some hurling their arrows hopelessly after each other, others stabbing into the sky like red-hot sparks, and the night was so illumined by them all that you could follow the smoke from the skillets of the hamburger joints high into the air before it disappeared into the darkness, along with the hot steam of the coffee urns. Amidst the acrid smell of burning molasses, before salt-water-taffy machines swaying rhythmically as they pulled the fat, creamy ribbons to and fro, girls opened cupid's-bow mouths to receive huge wobbling cones of cotton candy extended eagerly by their sailor boy friends. The ground shook beneath me with the thudding of thousands of feet on the wooden boardwalk, stained in spots from the wet footprints of late bathers and the spilled soda pop of boys my age who shook up the open bottles and released their thumbs to aim the spray at the unsuspecting before they fled. And over it all the intermittent roar of the plunging roller coaster across the way at Steeplechase Park, its electric controls rattling as it raced down below the horizon like an express train to hell.

Uncle Dan led the way to Nathan's hot-dog stand and said to a Greek counterman, "Two franks well done, Chris, for me and my nephew." He turned to me. "You take yours with sauerkraut? I forget."

I said boldly, "I like mine with everything." Mother would never have let me eat a spicy hot dog in the middle of the night, much less with all that junk smeared, rubbed, and squeezed on it.

"That's your nephew, hey, Doc?"

"Come in from the West to keep me company for a while. We're going to have some fun, us two bachelors." My uncle took a huge bite; I had never before seen anyone handle a hot dog, a cigar, and a toothpick all at once. "And listen, Chris, if this boy comes by with a hungry look during the day, his credit is good."

"I got you." The counterman extended his bare arm, hairy as a gorilla's. "Have a knish, kid."

We washed down the hot dogs and knishes with big shupers of root beer. The glass mugs were heavy as sin, frosty, with foam running down the sides; Uncle Dan blew off some of the suds at me as if we were drinking beer, which was just what I had been secretly pretending. As we strolled on he asked, "What time do they make you go to bed back home?"

I hesitated. I wanted to add thirty minutes to my weekend late limit, but then something made me answer honestly.

Uncle Dan screwed up his face. "That sounds awful damn early to me. At least, it is for Coney Island. Tell you what, if you promise not to snitch to your mother, we'll just forget that curfew stuff while you're staying with me."

I could hardly trust myself to reply.

"Your mother's a good woman," Uncle Dan remarked, in a thoughtful tone that I had never heard him use before. He took me by the elbow and led me to his apartment through the midnight crowds, thicker than we had even for circuses back home. "She's got her troubles, you know, like all of us. But she's my favorite. I mean, your uncles are all right, they're not bad fellows, but they've made a couple mistakes. Number one was when they got married."

As he threw away his cigar, he added, "Number two was when Al and Eddie left Brooklyn. In Manhattan, you don't even realize that you're living on the shore, on the edge of the ocean, the way you do here.

He fell silent, and I, matching my step to his, could not remember when Uncle Dan had ever talked to me so much all at once. After a while he went on, "This is a good place to live. You'll see…."

I did get a rather haphazard tourist's view of New York in the days that followed—waiting in line with the other out-of-towners on Sixth Avenue to see a Marlene Dietrich movie about the Russian Revolution at Radio City Music Hall, riding the elevator to the top of the Empire State Building to peer down at the tiny pedestrians who might be Uncle Al or Uncle Eddie ("from up here your uncles look like ants")—but what entered deep into my being was a sense of the variety and richness of possibility in the city, a sense of how one could, if one only wished, enter any of a number of communities, each as unique as the single one in the small town I had left behind.

Uncle Dan did this for me, and without even realizing it. All he knew was that it might be fun for me to tag along with him for a while. It never occurred to him that just by exposing me to his daily round, which to him was not particularly exciting but pleasant enough so that he had no deep incentive to change it, he was presenting me with motives for persisting in this confounding, fascinating world....

And in the course of that week I saw signs and portents, cabalic, symbols chalked on the city streets and tattooed on the shoulders of beings who ate cold steel; I rode with lunatics, moved from murderers to fallen woman, accepted an inscribed photo from the fattest woman in the world, and one morning Van Mungo, the great Dodger pitcher, my hero long before I had come to Brooklyn, and my uncle's friend, rumpled my hair and autographed a baseball for me to take home, where I could varnish it to protect his signature and display it to the doubters of Dunkirk.

What is more, during Uncle Dan's office hours I lolled on the beach with *Official Detective* magazines from his waiting room that were forbidden me at home, surrounded by the undressed throngs come in their thousands from every strifling flat in New York, from ever darkened corner of the world, actually, to sun themselves at my side; I learned the sweet subtleties of bluff and deception, kibitzing at the weekly session of my uncle's poker club, attended by the cadaverous dentist, Dr. Reinitz, and three Coney Island businessmen; and I was not just allowed but encouraged to stay up practically all night for the great flashy Mardi Gras parade, blinking sleepy-eyed at the red rows of fire engines rolling glossily along streets sparkling like Catherine wheels. It was the greatest week of my life.

COUPLE AT CONEY ISLAND

CHARLES SIMIC

It was early one Sunday morning,
So we put on our best rags
And went for a stroll along the boardwalk
Till we came to a kind of palace
With turrets and pennants flying.
It made me think of a wedding cake
In the window of a fancy bakery shop.

I was warm, so I took my jacket off
And put my arm round your waist
And drew you closer to me
While you leaned your head on my shoulder,
Anyone could see we'd made love
The night before and were still giddy on our feet.
We looked naked in our clothes

Staring at the red and white pennants
Whipped by the sea wind.
The rides and shooting galleries
With their ducks marching in line
Still boarded up and padlocked.
No one around yet to take our first dime.

ICE CREAM CONES

*T*here is some controversy about who created the first ice cream cone. In 1896 Italian immigrant Italo Marchiony, who sold his homemade ice cream from a pushcart on Wall Street, baked edible waffle cups to avoid customers breaking or stealing the serving dishes. In 1903, he was issued a patent for his invention. In 1904, Ernest Hamwi of Syria exhibited a similar creation at the 1904 St. Louis World's Fair. Hamwi was selling a crispy waffle-like pastry called zalabis in a booth next to a popular ice cream vendor. As the vendor ran out of dishes, Hamwi came to the rescue by rolling one of his waffle pastries in the shape of a cone, letting it cool, and filling it with ice cream.

During the summer of 1790, George Washington reportedly ran up a $200 tab at an ice cream parlor on Chatham Street. Thomas Andreas Carvelas of Yonkers, who shortened his name to Tom Carvel, invented a machine that created frozen custard which he sold from a truck on the streets of New York City. In 1960, Polish immigrant Reuben Mattus invented Häagen-Dazs ice cream, which had high butterfat content and very little air. The first three flavors were vanilla, chocolate, and coffee.

ICE CREAM CONES

ICE CREAM CONES
3/4 cup granulated sugar

1 large egg

2 tablespoons butter, melted and cooled

1 teaspoon vanilla extract

1/4 cup milk

1/2 cup all-purpose flour, sifted

This is a basic recipe that can be altered in several ways. You can purchase a cone-shaped mold at a specialty food store if you want to get fancy. You can also follow this recipe and lay the cookie into a bowl for an ice-cream bowl. Another variation involves using a waffle iron to cook the cookies quickly, watching to see when they turn golden, and then molding them into a cone or bowl. Make 'em big, make 'em small, make 'em round, make 'em tall—it's up to you.

This recipe is also aided greatly by a "Silpat," a durable cover for a cookie sheet that makes removal MUCH easier and cooking more even. (They are available at most specialty stores).

ICE CREAM CONES

1. Before you begin making the cookies, make or purchase a 6-inch-round stencil to use in shaping the cookies. They can be made easily and inexpensively by tracing two or three 6-inch circles onto a piece of wax paper. Using a sharp knife or exacto blade, cut out the circle without disturbing the rest of the paper. Lay the stencil cut-out on top of your Silpat or cookie sheet and you have a guide that can but moved, reused, and tossed out when you're finished.

2. Preheat oven to 300° F.

3. In a mixing bowl, beat the sugar and egg with an electric mixer until they are a pale yellow. Beat in the butter, vanilla, and milk. Gradually stir in the flour.

4. Grease a large non-stick cookie sheet and spread 2 tablespoons of the batter into your 6-inch stencil hole using a thin, flexible spatula.

5. Bake for 15 minutes or until lightly browned. Remove each cookie from the sheet and wrap around a cone-shaped mold (if making cones), sealing the point at the bottom. If making bowls, simply slide the cookies from the sheet to a clean bowl in your desired shape and allow to cool. The cookies harden as they cool so work as quickly as you can.

6. Top with your favorite ice cream.

Makes 8 to 10 cones.

THE 'HOODS

In the comics, Peter Parker, Spider-Man's alter ego, grew up at 20 Ingram Street, a boarding house run by his Aunt May in the heart of Forest Hills Gardens. The address actually exists and is home to a family named Parker.

Although Truman Capote's name is synonymous with the glamour of Manhattan, it was in his basement apartment at 70 Willow Street in Brooklyn Heights that Capote wrote *Breakfast at Tiffany's* and *In Cold Blood*.

Charles Lewis Tiffany opened his jewelry store on lower Broadway in 1837 with $1,000 borrowed from his father. In its first week, the store racked up a profit of 33 cents.

Edgar Allan Poe was already a noted literary critic, poet and author in 1846 when he rented a small cottage in Fordham in the Bronx for $100 a year. He hoped the fresh air would cure his wife's tuberculosis. He wrote *Annabel Lee* and *The Bells* there.

In 1842, Samuel Morse laid the first telegraph cable between the Battery and Governor's Island. It was snapped by a ship's anchor.

✻

On November 1, 1683, the British formed Kings and Queens Counties, naming the regions in honor of England's King Charles II and his wife, Catherine of Braganza.

✻

A ride on the Cyclone at Coney Island lasts exactly one minute and 50 seconds.

✻

The Lincoln Memorial may be in Washington, D.C., but it was made in the Bronx. The Piccirilli brothers of Pisa carved the statue in their studio there from a design by Daniel Chester French.

✻

Brooklyn's Atlantic Avenue, today a center for Middle Eastern markets, was formerly referred to as "Swedish Broadway."

✻

What Manhattan subway station has a beaver mosaic? Astor Place does, because the Astors made their fortune in the beaver hunting trade.

✻

Battery Park City is built on a landfill created from 1.2 million cubic yards of earth and rock excavated from the site of the World Trade Center in the 1960s.

✻

Marilyn Monroe filmed the famous dress-blowing scene in "The Seven Year Itch" on 52nd and Lexington.

✻

Coney Island was named after the Dutch word "coney," which means rabbit, because the area was overrun with rabbits.

✻

On June 12, 1839, the town of Sunswik was renamed Astoria to butter-up millionaire John Jacob Astor to fund a women's college; it was never built, but the name stuck.

A&P Supermarkets, the largest
chain store in the world, began
on Vesey Street in 1859 as
The Atlantic & Pacific Tea Company.

Peter Luger's Brooklyn restaurant
serves up 10 tons of steak a week.

Love Lane, located in Brooklyn Heights,
is part of an ancient American
Indian trail that led to the East River.

Brooklyn was settled in 1636,
and chartered as part of New York
City in 1898. From Dutch and Walloon
settlements it became the village
of Brooklyn Ferry in 1816, and
then the city of Brooklyn in 1834.

The oldest surviving schoolhouse in the
United States, built in 1695, is in Staten
Island's historic Richmond Town.

The Sandy Ground Historical Society
is the oldest continuously inhabited
settlement established by free
black slaves in North America.

The Bronx was settled in 1639 and is named
for the Swedish settler Jonas Bronck.

Bronx's Woodlawn cemetery is
the final resting place of Duke
Ellington and Miles Davis.

The Manhattan House of Detention,
known as the Tombs, was built in lower
Manhattan in the 1830s. About 50,000
prisoners pass through it annually.

And New York is the most beautiful city
in the world? It is not far from it. No urban night is like the
night there....Squares after squares of flame, set up
and cut into the ether. Here is our poetry,
for we have pulled down the stars to our will.

EZRA POUND

THE GREAT FIGURE

William Carlos Williams

Among the rain
and lights
I saw a figure 5
in gold
on a red
firetruck
moving
tense
unheeded
to gong clangs
siren howls
and wheels rumbling
through the dark city.

283

NEW YORK–STYLE CHEESECAKE

*N*ew York cheesecake evolved from an Eastern European–style cake made from a combination of cream cheese and pot cheese, now called cottage cheese. Cheesecake is believed to have originated in ancient Greece and was served to the athletes during the first Olympic Games in 776 B.C. In 1872, cream cheese was invented by American dairymen, who were trying to recreate the French Neufchâtel cheese. Arnold Reuben Jr., a descendant of German immigrants, claimed that his family developed the first cream cheese cake recipe and in 1929 Reuben's cheesecake won a gold medal at the New York World's Fair. By 1949, Lindy's in the theater district, owned by Leo Linderman, is credited with making the New York cheesecake famous.

CRUST

CRUST
2 cups (20 crackers)
cinnamon graham
crackers

5 tablespoons
granulated sugar

6 tablespoons melted
unsalted butter

1. Preheat oven to 350° F.

2. Place graham crackers in a blender or food processor and grind into crumbs. Alternatively, you can place them in a zip-lock baggie and roll them with a rolling pin.

3. Combine crumbs, sugar, and melted butter. Press mixture along the bottom and sides of springform pan.

4. Bake for 8–10 minutes and allow to cool slightly.

NEW YORK–STYLE CHEESECAKE

FILLING

32 ounces cream cheese, at room temperature

1 2/3 cups granulated sugar

1/4 cup cornstarch

1 tablespoon vanilla extract

2 extra-large eggs

3/4 cup heavy whipping cream

TOPPING

12 ounces sour cream

2 tablespoons granulated sugar

CHEESECAKE

1. Preheat oven to 350° F.

2. Place one 8-ounce package of cream cheese, 1/3 cup sugar, and cornstarch in a large bowl and beat on low until smooth. Increase speed to high and add remaining cream cheese and vanilla.

3. Add eggs, one at a time. Finally, add heavy cream and zest. Beat only until combined. Do not overmix.

4. Pour mixture into prepared crust.

5. Place the springform pan in a large shallow pan containing hot water that comes about 1-inch up the sides of the pan. Tent with tin foil.

6. Bake the cheesecake until the center barely jiggles when you shake the pan, about 1 hour.

7. Refrigerate at least 4 hours.

8. Combine sour cream and sugar. Spread evenly over cheesecake and refrigerate at least one hour more. Slice and serve.

GIVE MY REGARDS TO BROADWAY

George M. Cohan

Did you ever see two Yankees part upon
  a foreign shore,
When the good ship's just about to start
  for Old New York once more?
With tear-dimmed eye they say good-bye,
they're friends without a doubt;
When the man on the pier
Shouts, "Let them clear," as the ship
  strikes out.

Give my regards to Broadway,
remember me to Herald Square,
Tell all the gang at Forty-Second street,
that I will soon be there;

Whisper of how I'm yearning,
To mingle with the old time throng,
give my regards to old Broadway
and say that I'll be there e'er long.

Say hello to dear old Coney Isle, if there
  you chance to be,
When you're at the Waldorf have a smile
  and charge it up to me;
Mention my name ev'ry place you go,
as 'round the town you roam;
Wish you'd call on my gal,
Now remember, old pal,
when you get back home.

Give my regards to Broadway,
remember me to Herald Square,
Tell all the gang at Forty-Second street,
that I will soon be there;

Whisper of how I'm yearning,
To mingle with the old time throng,
give my regards to old Broadway
and say that I'll be there e'er long.

MOVIES

CLASSICS

An Affair to Remember (1957): A playboy and a night-club singer have an affair on a cruise to New York, but their planned reunion at the Empire State Building is prevented by circumstance.

Breakfast at Tiffany's (1961): A struggling writer living off a rich, older woman, and his neighbor, a would-be socialite living off the favors of rich men, find something neither of them expected: each other.

King Kong (1933): A giant gorilla is captured on a tropical island and brought to New York for display, but soon escapes.

Miracle on 34th Street (1947): In this classic Christmas tale, a young girl convinces New York that the Macy's Department Store Santa is, in fact, the real Santa Claus.

A Night at the Opera (1935): The Marx Brothers try to land an important gig for their friend, a talented, unknown opera singer.

West Side Story (1961): An Italian gang member falls in love with the sister of a rival Puerto Rican gang member in this musical remake of William Shakespeare's *Romeo and Juliet*.

COMEDIES

Annie Hall (1979): Writer/Director/Star Woody Allen explores and analyzes relationships through the story of the roller coaster romance between a comedian and his ex-girlfriend.

Arthur (1981): Arthur is a loveable, lazy drunk who will only receive his rather sizeable inheritance if he agrees to marry Susan, a woman he doesn't love.

Barefoot in the Park (1967): A newlywed couple try to adapt to married life in a five-story walkup in New York.

Ghostbusters (1984): Four supernatural investigators calling themselves the Ghostbusters fight to save the world from the wrath of an ancient Sumerian god.

Tootsie (1982): A difficult, struggling actor finds that the only way he can get work is by dressing as a woman.

Trading Places (1983): A rich businessman and a small-time hood find themselves living one another's lifestyle as a result of a bet between two powerful commodity brokers.

When Harry Met Sally (1989): Harry and Sally search for love while trying to maintain a platonic friendship, even though they start falling for each other.

MUSIC AND DANCE

All That Jazz (1979): Legendary Broadway choreographer Bob Fosse directs this brutally honest, auto-biographical movie about a Broadway dancer's compulsive indulgences in drugs, sex and on the stage.

The Cotton Club (1984): Period film centering on the legendary Cotton Club, of jazz fame, and the tensions of race and crime which surrounded it.

Fame (1980): Four students look for success as they train in the New York High School for the Performing Arts.

Ragtime (1981): A look into the history, people, and rhythms of the Ragtime era through the story of a black piano player seeking vengeance on a group of men who attacked him.

Saturday Night Fever (1977): Tony, a tough, uneducated youth with a passion for dancing, tries to make a name for himself on the disco floor.

DRAMA

The Age of Innocence (1993): Socialite Newland Archer sees his life turned upside-down as he falls for his fiancée's cousin in this tale of 19th century New York.

The Basketball Diaries (1995): The true story of high school basketball star Jim Carroll's descent into heroin addiction.

The Godfather (1972): After an assassination attempt on Vito Corleone, the most powerful mob boss in New York, his son Michael sparks a mob war by murdering his father's enemy.

Kramer vs. Kramer (1979): A divorced man struggles to adapt to life on his own while battling for the custody of his son.

Smoke (1995): A neighborhood's story is told through the comings and goings of customers at Auggie's Smoke Shop.

Taxi Driver (1976): A disturbed, insomniac taxi driver makes it his mission to save a 13-year-old prostitute by any means.

HORROR AND SUSPENSE

King Kong (1976): In this remake of the 1933 classic, a petroleum company expedition to a tropical island yields an unexpected discovery: a monstrous gorilla.

Rosemary's Baby (1968): When Rosemary and her husband move into a new apartment building, supernatural things start to happen all around them, and Rosemary suspects that her new pregnancy may be one of them.

The Fisher King (1991): A radio talk show host forms a relationship with a strange homeless man who claims to be searching for the Holy Grail.

The Thomas Crown Affair (1999): A bored millionaire's only passion is pulling off challenging heists of priceless art. But now a pretty detective is on to him.

METROPOLIS

JEROME CHARYN

NEW YORK WAS PRACTICAL AND INSANE....It decided to grow along a grid, ignoring bumps, ditches, and heights, and the particular bend of its rivers. It would be a phantom grid of 2028 blocks, where anything that was built upon them could be removed at will. So we have the Empire State Building dug into the old cradle of the Waldorf-Astoria. And the Waldorf is shoved onto another grid. We have a Madison Square Garden on Madison Square and then the Garden starts to float, like a gondola on the grid. It reappears uptown, caters to circuses and rodeos, the Rangers and the Knicks, becomes a parking lot, and the Garden is born again over the new Penn Station. It's an ugly glass tank, but who cares? Nothing is sacred except the grid. And the grid doesn't allow for memory and remorse.

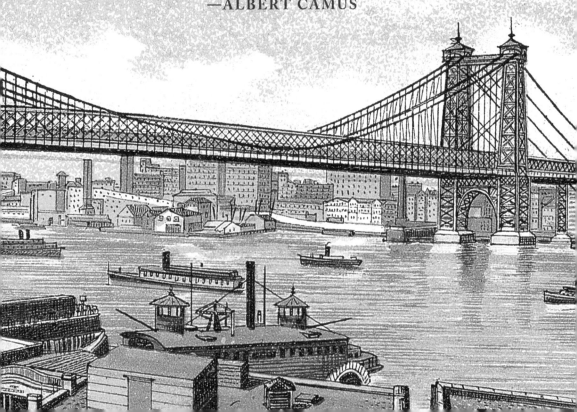

Sometimes, from beyond the skyscrapers, the cry of a tugboat finds you in your insomnia, and you remember that this desert of iron and cement is an island.

—ALBERT CAMUS

PHOTOGRAPH FROM SEPTEMBER 11

WISLAWA SZYMBORSKA

They jumped from the burning floors—
one, two, a few more,
higher, lower.

The photograph halted them in life,
and now keeps them
above the earth toward the earth.

Each is still complete,
with a particular face
and blood well-hidden.

There's enough time
for hair to come loose,
for keys and coins
to fall from pockets.

They're still within the air's reach,
in the compass of places
that have just now opened.

I can do only two things for them—
describe this flight
and not add a last line.

THE LUNGS

JAMES HUNEKER

I POSITIVELY REFUSE TO SING the praises of Central Park—which was laid out in 1857 (avaunt, statistics!)—simply because that once haughty and always artificial dame is fast becoming an old lady in plain decadence. Who has not sung her praises! Hardly a park, rather a cluster of graceful arboreal arabesques, which surprise and charm, Central Park is, nevertheless, moribund, and all the king's horses and all the king's men can never set her up again in her former estate. The city itself has assassinated her, not by official neglect, but by the proximity of stone, steel, and brick, which is slowly robbing her of her sustenance of earth, air, and moisture.

In the first flush of spring or a few early summer days she wears her old smile of brightness. How welcome the leafy arch of the Mall, how impressive, how "European" the vista of the Bethesda fountain, the terrace, and the lake; how pleasing it is to sit under the arbor of the Casion piazza and watch the golden girls and slim gilt lads arrive in motor-cars!

Then the Ramble, or the numerous bypaths that lead to the reservoir, or that give on the bridle-paths, wherein joyous youth

with grooms flit by, or prosperous cits showing lean, crooked shanks painfully bump on horses too wide for them. Ah, yes! Central Park will continue for years to furnish amusement (if that wretched Zoo were only banished to the Bronx!) and deep breathing for the lucky rider who lives on its borders. Also furnish fun for May parties, June walks, and July depredations. It is a miracle of landscape-gardening, notwithstanding its absence of monotony—it abounds in too many twists and turns; it is seldom reposeful, because broad meadows are absent. You can't do much in decoration without flat surfaces. But what mortal could accomplish what Frederick Law Olmsted and Calvert Vaux accomplished; the impending ruin is the result of pitiless natural causes.

I once said that one can't be a flâneur in a city without trees. New York is almost treeless, and Central Park soon will be. When not so long ago I saluted the Obelisk on the Thames embankment, that antique and morose stylite sent its regards to its brother in our Park. Some day when the last Yankee (the breed is rapidly running out) will look at the plans of what was once Central Park, hanging in the Metropolitan Museum, his eye will caress the Obelisk across the way. That strange shaft will endure when New York is become an abomination and a desolation.

Arthur Brisbane's notion that the nasty little lakes and water pools be drained and refilled with salt water for bathing purposes is a capital one. Gone at a swoop malaria and evil odors; gone, too, the mosquitoes which make life miserable for nigh dwellers. But the park is doomed; let us enjoy its ancient bravery while we may.

I never skated at Van Cortlandt Park, because I can't skate; but I love the spot, love the old mansion and its relics, love the open felling about it. Atop of the highest part of the island is Isham Park. To reach it get off at the Two Hundred and Seventh Street Subway station and walk westwardly up the hill, or through Isham Street. On the brow is the little park, looking up and down the Hudson and across Spuyten Duyvil. A rare spot to watch airplane races. Not far away is the Billings castle, and across the Fort Washington Road the studio and Gothic cloisters of the sculptor George Grey Barnars.

Often have I enjoyed the Zoological Garden in the Bronx, the Botanical Garden, and the Bronx Park. Our Zoo is easily the largest and most complete in the world. I've visited all the European Zoos, from Amsterdam and Hamburg to Vienna and Budapest. As for the Botanical Garden, I have the famous botanist Hugo de Vries of Amsterdam as a witness, who told me he would be happy to live near it always.

*A*ny fool can stand upon a hill in the country and be aware that grass is up and trees have begun to bud; but in the city spring is served a la carte rather than in heaping portions. Back on my farm lie heavy woods, yet none of these trees appeals to me so deeply as a scrubby sapling which grew in the back yard of my house in New York— when a tree digs its roots down among water pipes and gas mains and thrusts its way up through dust and cinders, that's something. I sometimes think that never blooms a tulip quite so red as that which shows its head in a Park Avenue flower bed between the traffic. We Manhattan nature lovers love her best because we know so little about her.

—HEYWOOD BROUN

I GO ADVENTURING

HELEN KELLER

CUT OFF AS I AM, it is inevitable that I should sometimes feel like a shadow walking in a shadowy world. When this happens I ask to be taken to New York City. Always I return home weary but I have the comforting certainty that mankind is real flesh and I myself am not a dream.

In order to get to New York from my home it is necessary to cross one of the great bridges that separate Manhattan from Long Island. The oldest and most interesting of them is the Brooklyn Bridge, built by my friend, Colonel Roebling, but the one I cross oftenest is the Queensborough Bridge at 59th Street. How often I have had Manhattan described to me from these bridges! They tell me the view is loveliest in the morning and at sunset when one sees the skyscrapers rising like fairy palaces, their million windows gleaming in the rosy-tinted atmosphere.

I like to feel that all poetry is not between the covers of poetry books, that much of it is written in great enterprises of engineering and flying, that into mighty utility man has poured and is pouring his dreams, his emotions, his philosophy. This materializing of his genius is sometimes inchoate and monstrous, but even then sublime in its extravagance and courage. Who can deny that the Queensborough Bridge is the work of a creative artist? It never fails to give me a poignant desire to capture the noble cadence of its music. To my friends I say:

Behold its liberal loveliness of length—
A flowing span from shore to shore,
A brimming reach of beauty matched with strength,
It shines and climbs like some miraculous dream,
Like some vision multitudinous and agleam,
A passion of desire held captive in the clasp of vast utility.

New York has a special interest for me when it is wrapped in fog. Then it behaves very much like a blind person. I once crossed from Jersey City to Manhattan in a dense fog. The ferry-boat felt its way cautiously through the river traffic. More timid than a blind man, its horn brayed incessantly. Fog-bound, surrounded by menacing, unseen craft and dangers, it halted every now and then as a blind man halts at a crowded thoroughfare crossing, tapping his cane, tense and anxious.

One of my never-to-be-forgotten experiences was circum-navigating New York in a boat. The trip took all day. I had with me four people who could use the hand alphabet—my teacher, my sister, my niece, and Mr. Holmes. One who has not seen New York in this way would be amazed at the number of people who live on the water. Someone has called them "harbor gypsies." Their homes are on boats—whole fleets of them, decorated with flower boxes and bright-colored awnings. It is amusing to note how many of these stumbling, awkward harbor gypsies have pretty feminine names—*Bella*, *Floradora*,

308

Rosalind, Pearl of the Deep, Minnehaha, Sister Nell. The occupants can be seen going about their household tasks—cooking, washing, sewing, gossiping from one barge to another, and there is a flood of smells which gives eyes to the mind. The children and dogs play on the tiny deck, and chase each other into the water, where they are perfectly at home. These water-babies are familiar with all manner of craft, they know what countries they come from, and what cargoes they carry. There are brick barges from Holland and fruitboats coming in from Havana, and craft loaded with meat, cobblestones, and sand push their way up bays and canals. There are old ships which have been stripped of their majesty and doomed to follow tow ropes up and down the harbor. These ships make me think of old blind people led up and down the city streets. There are aristocratic craft from Albany, Nyack, Newburg. There are also boats from New London and Boston, from the Potomac and Baltimore and Virginia, from Portland, Maine, bringing terra cotta to Manhattan. Here comes the fishing fleet from Gloucester hurrying past the barge houses, and crawling, coal-laden tramps. Tracking the turmoil in every direction are the saucy ferry boats, bellowing rudely to everyone to get out of the way.

It is a sail of vivid contrast—up the Hudson between green hills, past the stately mansions of Riverside Drive, through the narrow straits that separate Manhattan from the mainland, into

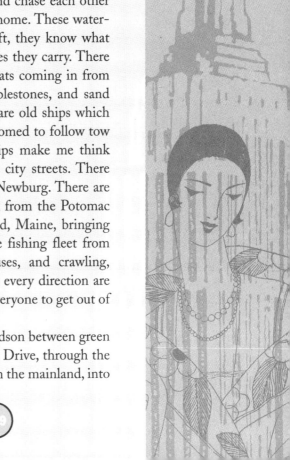

Harlem and the East River, past Welfare Island, where a great modern city shelters its human derelicts, on to the welter of downtown docks, where longshoremen heave the barge cargoes ashore, and the crash of traffic is deafening, and back to your pier in the moonlight when the harbor gypsies sleep and the sense of peace is balm to the tired nerves.

As I walk up Broadway, the people that brush past me seem always hastening toward a destination they never reach. Their motions are eager, as if they said, "We are on our way, we shall arrive in a moment." They keep up the pace—they almost run. Each on his quest intent, in endless procession they pass, tragic, grotesque, gay, they all sweep onward like rain falling upon leaves. I wonder where they are going. I puzzle my brain; but the mystery is never solved. Will they at last come somewhere? Will anybody be waiting for them? The march never ceases. Their feet have worn the pavements unevenly. I wish I knew where they are going. Some are nonchalant, some walk with their eyes on the ground, others step lightly, as if they might fly if their wings were not bound by the multitude. A pale little woman is guiding the steps of a blind man. His great hand drags on her arm. Awkwardly he shortens his stride to her gait. He trips when the curb is uneven; his grip tightens on the arm of the woman. Where are they going?

Like figures in a meaningless pageant, they pass. There are young girls laughing, loitering. They have beauty, youth, lovers. They look in the shop windows, they look at the huge winking signs; they jostle the crowds, their feet keep time to the music of their hearts. They must be going to a pleasant place. I think I should like to go where they are going.

Tremulously I stand in the subways, absorbed into the terrible reverberations of exploding energy. Fearful, I touch the forest of steel girders loud with the thunder of oncoming trains that shoot past me like projectiles. Inert I stand, riveted in my place. My limbs, paralyzed, refuse to obey the will insistent on haste to board the train while the lightning steed is leashed and its reeling speed checked for a moment. Before my mind flashes in clairvoyant vision what all this speed portends—the lightning crashing into life, the accidents, railroad wrecks, steam bursting free like geysers from bands of steel, thousands of racing motors and children caught at play, flying heroes diving into the sea, dying for speed—all this because of strange, unsatisfied ambitions. Another train bursts into the station like a volcano, the people crowd me on, on into the chasm—into the dark depths of awful forces and fates. In a few minutes, still trembling, I am spilled into the streets.

LETTER TO N.Y.

ELIZABETH BISHOP

In your next letter I wish you'd say
where you are going and what you are doing;
how are the plays, and after the plays
what other pleasures you're pursuing:

taking cabs in the middle of the night,
driving as if to save your soul
where the road goes round and round the park
and the meter glares like a moral owl,

and the trees look so queer and green
standing alone in big black caves
and suddenly you're in a different place
where everything seems to happen in waves,

and most of the jokes you just can't catch,
like dirty words rubbed off a slate,
and the songs are loud but somehow dim
and it gets so terribly late,

and coming out of the brownstone house
to the gray sidewalk, the watered street,
one side of the buildings rises with the sun
like a glistening field of wheat.

—Wheat, not oats, dear. I'm afraid
if its wheat its none of your sowing,
nevertheless I'd like to know
what you are doing and where you are going.

THEME FROM NEW YORK, NEW YORK

Fred Ebb

Start spreadin' the news,
I'm leaving today,
I wanna be a part of it
New York, New York.

These vagabond shoes
are longing to stray,
And step around the heart of it
New York, New York.

I wanna wake up in the city
    that doesn't sleep
to find I'm king of the hill,
top of the heap.

My little town blues
are melting away,
I'll make a brand new start of it
in old New York.

If I can make it there,
I'd make it anywhere,
It's up to you,
New York, New York.

king of the hill,
head of the list,
cream of the crop at the top
    of the heap.
My little town blues
are melting away,
I'll make a brand new start of it
in old New York.

If I can make it there
I'd make it anywhere,
Come on, come through
New York, New York.

$\mathcal{A}$t night…the streets become rhythmical perspectives of glowing dotted lines, reflections hung upon them in the streets as the wisteria hangs its violet racemes on its trellis. The buildings are shimmering verticality, a gossamer veil, a festive scene-prop hanging there against the black sky to dazzle, entertain, amaze.

—FRANK LLOYD WRIGHT

ARCHITECTURE

Trinity Church, at the intersection of Broadway and Wall Street, was New York's tallest building during the 19th century, standing 284 feet tall. It was used as a beacon for ships coming into New York harbor.

The Wyckoff House in Brooklyn, built around 1652, is the oldest house in New York City.

The trading area of the New York Stock Exchange is about two-thirds the size of a football field.

The Williamsburg Bridge was initially built just for subways. In the 1920s it carried 500,000 people to Manhattan daily. Once cars were allowed, the full capacity decreased and could only accommodate 250,000 people per day by car and train.

The world's largest gothic cathedral is the Cathedral Church of St. John the Divine, and it is still under construction. Its first stone was laid in 1892.

Olana is the Persian-style home and picturesque landscape created by Frederic Edwin Church, one of the most renowned American artists of the Hudson River School. Begun in 1870, the castle-like structure took two years to build. Over forty years, Church transformed 250 acres of treeless farm fields into an artistic composition encompassing a lake, a park, the grounds immediately surrounding the house, a farm, an extensive road system, and superlative views of the Catskill Mountains and the Hudson River.

Donald Trump's first big deal was converting the old Commodore Hotel, next to Grand Central Terminal, into the glittery Grand Hyatt in 1980, complete with gold Mylar tablecloths.

The first building in New York constructed specifically as a tenement is at 65 Mott Street, near Pell Street.

The lions at the New York Public Library were originally named Leo Astor and Leo Lenox, after the library's two founders. They are now known as Patience and Fortitude, nicknames given them by former mayor La Guardia.

There are 53 major bridges in the five boroughs of New York City.

PRETZELS

1 cup lukewarm water
1 tablespoon yeast
4 tablespoons brown sugar
2 teaspoons sea salt
3 cups all-purpose flour
1 tablespoon baking soda dissolved in 1 cup boiling water
1 egg beaten with 1 teaspoon water in a small bowl
Coarse sea salt

*T*he wafting scent of hot, doughy, salty pretzels emanating from a street vendor's cart is the smell of a New York City street. The pretzel is an historic food, first created sometime around 610 AD, when monks in northern Italy or southern France were playing around with some leftover strips of bread, and twisted and folded them to resemble arms folded over the chest in prayer. The baked treats were then given to children who studied their prayers. The bread was called "pretiola," which means "little reward" or "little prayers" in Latin. Nowadays, pretzels are the second most popular snack food after potato chips. In New York City, you can find a street pretzel vendor on hundreds of corners, making it the perfect noshing food. Don't forget the mustard!

1. Preheat oven to 425° F.

2. Mix water, yeast, brown sugar and salt in a large mixing bowl. Add flour and knead until dough is smooth (about 3 minutes). Allow dough to rest in refrigerator, covered, for at least one hour, but preferably overnight.

3. Divide the dough into 6 or 12 pieces. Roll each piece into a long thin rope, like you were making a snake out of clay.

4. Shape each section into an upside down U-shape in front of you. Bring the ends together and twist them halfway up, making them look like a tie or ribbon.

5. Flatten the loose ends with your fingers and bring to the top of the pretzel (the top of the upside-down U) and press into the dough to secure it. It should look like a pretzel by now.

6. Place on a greased cookie sheet.

7. Let the pretzels rise for 30 minutes or when about double in size. Brush with the water–baking soda solution followed by the egg wash.

8. Sprinkle generously with coarse salt.

9. Bake for 12 to 15 minutes or until golden brown.

10. Serve hot with stone ground mustard.

Makes 6 large or 12 small pretzels.

Situated on an island which I think it will one day cover, it rises like Venice from the sea, and like that fairest of cities in the days of her glory, receives into its lap tribute of all the riches of the earth.
—FRANCES TROLLOPE

LAKE PLACID

Lake Placid is one of only three communities to host two Winter Olympics (1932 and 1980). The other two are Innsbruck, Austria and St. Moritz, Switzerland.

During the 1980 Olympic games in Lake Placid, the U.S. Hockey team defeated the Soviet Union by a score of 4–3 in what is considered one of the greatest moments in sports history—often referred to as "The Miracle on Ice."

Port Henry was the largest pre-war producer of iron ore in the country, flourishing from 1820 to 1971.

At the 1932 Winter Olympics in Lake Placid, Sonja Henie, *aka* the "Norwegian Doll," figure skated her way to her second of three consecutive Olympic gold medals, a feat that has never been equaled.

Historic Fort Ticonderoga on Lake Champlain is the site of major victories in the Seven Years' War and the American Revolution.

The Adirondack Park is the largest state park in the U.S., covering six million acres—an area larger than the Grand Canyon, Yellowstone, and Yosemite combined.

Four of New York State's natural wonders are in Lake Placid: Ausable Chasm, High Falls Gorge, Howe Caverns, and Natural Stone Ridge and Caves.

Saranac Lake is widely known for its 1880s "Cure Cottages," which were created when the area became a major treatment center for tuberculosis. Several large sanatorium complexes were built around Saranac Lake, many of which are still standing today.

Lake Placid has hosted an Ironman Triathalon since 1999. It features a 2.4-mile swim, a 112-mile bike, and a full marathon (26.2 miles)— all to be completed within 17 hours.

In 1980, the Austrians were so confident of winning the Alpine ski championship that they erected a building—the "Austria Haus"— in which to celebrate their victories. Luckily, they won four gold metals.

*I*t wasn't until I got to New York that I became Kansan. Everyone there kept reminding me that they were Jewish or Irish, or whatever, so I kept reminding them that I was midwestern. Before I knew it, I actually began to brag about being from Kansas! I discovered that I had something a bit unique, but it was the nature of New York that forced me to claim my past.

—WILLIAM INGE

NIAGARA FALLS

In 1985 Steven Trotter became the youngest man to conquer the crest of Niagara Falls in two plastic pickle barrels surrounded by rubber inner tubes.

More water flows over Niagara Falls every year than over any other waterfall on the planet (600,000 U.S. gallons per second).

Niagara Falls is the second largest falls in the world after Victoria Falls in Africa.

One fifth of the fresh water in the world lies in the four upper Great Lakes—Michigan, Huron, Superior, and Erie. The outflow empties into the Niagara River and eventually cascades over the falls.

Since 1901, 15 people have dared going over the falls in a barrel.

The first person to survive such a stunt was a 63-year-old female schoolteacher.

In 1960, a seven-year-old boy named Roger Woodward was swept over the falls after a boating accident and survived with minor injuries. He is the first person known to go over the falls without any protection—and live.

Niagara Falls has been a popular spot to honeymoon for more than 200 years. Jerome Bonaparte, Napoleon's younger brother, celebrated his recent marriage there in 1805.

High wire tightrope acts used to be performed across the river. Most notable was "Blondin," who once carried his manager across on his back, stopping midway to rest!

The word "Niagara" comes from the Iroquois word "Onguiaahra" meaning "the strait."

The Falls have never completely frozen over, but the flow was once halted over both falls on March 30, 1848 for 30 hours due to an ice jam in the upper river. Hundreds of people scoured the riverbed looking for souvenirs.

On June 10, 1996, the Sheraton Fallsview Hotel's Fallscam introduced a 24hr/day live shot of the Niagara Falls. Since then more than 30 million people have visited the site.

New York is like a country, the neighborhood is your town, you spot someone from the block or the building in another neighborhood and the first impulse to the brain is, What are *you* doing here?

—VIVIAN GORNICK

A HAZARD OF
NEW FORTUNES

WILLIAM DEAN HOWELLS

A T THIRD AVENUE they took the elevated, for which she confessed an infatuation. She declared it the most ideal way of getting about in the world, and was not ashamed when he reminded her of how she used to say that nothing under the sun could induce her to travel on it. She now said that the night transit was even more interesting than the day, and that the fleeting intimacy you formed with people in second and third floor interiors, while all the usual street life went on underneath, had a domestic intensity mixed with a perfect repose that was the last effect of good society with all its security and exclusiveness. He said it was better than the theatre, of which it reminded him, to see those people through their windows: a family party of work-folk at a late tea, some of the men in their shirt sleeves; a woman sewing by a lamp; a mother laying her child in its cradle; a man with his head fallen on his hands upon a table; a girl and her lover leaning

over the window-sill together. What suggestion! what drama! what infinite interest! At the Forty-second Street station they stopped a minute on the bridge that crosses the track to the branch road for the Central Depot, and looked up and down the long stretch of the elevated to north and south. The track that found and lost itself a thousand times in the flare and tremor of the innumerable lights; the moony sheen of the electrics mixing with the reddish points and blots of gas far and near; the architectural shapes of houses and churches and towers, rescued by the obscurity from all that was ignoble in them, and the coming and going of the trains marking the stations with vivider or fainter plumes of flame-shot steam— formed an incomparable perspective. They often talked afterward of the superb spectacle, which in a city full of painters nightly works its unrecorded miracles....

...she promised to write as soon as she reached home. She promised also that having seen the limitations of New York in respect to flats, she would not be hard on him if he took something not quite ideal. Only he must remember that it was not to be above Twentieth Street nor below Washington Square; it must not be higher than the third floor; it must have an elevator, steam heat, hall boys, and a pleasant janitor. These were essentials; if he could not get them, then they must do without. But he must get them.

BIZARRE AND INTERESTING, BUT TRUE

Oneida, New York is the home of the world's smallest church measuring 3.5 feet by 6 feet. Erected in 1989, this church is just big enough to hold a bride, groom, and minister.

Goldie Hawn's career began in a stint at the 1964–65 New York World's Fair in Flushing Meadow Park as a can-can dancer in the chorus at the Texas Pavilion.

Poet Dylan Thomas died at Greenwich Village's White Horse Tavern after proclaiming that he had just consumed 18 straight whiskies.

The nation's largest Halloween parade is the Greenwich Village Halloween Parade, held at night on October 31st.

Landscape architect Frederick Law Olmstead, who designed Central Park and Prospect Park, died in 1903 in McLean Psychiatric Hospital, Massachusetts. Olmstead had designed the grounds of this institution.

As late as the 1840s, thousands of pigs roamed Wall Street to consume garbage—an early sanitation system.

Each year the village of Chittenango, New York, celebrates the birth of L. Frank Baum, author of *The Wizard of Oz*. It's a weekend of games, rides, crafts, live entertainment, costume judging, and a huge parade featuring original Munchkins from the 1939 movie. Chittenango features a yellow brick inlaid sidewalk leading to Auntie Em's and other Oz-themed businesses.

On August 7, 1974 the French tightrope artist Philippe Petit walked a tightrope between the Twin Towers' tops, a distance of 131 feet. It took 45 minutes.

In 1908 *The New York Herald* installed a giant searchlight among the girders of the MetLife Tower, directly across from Madison Square Park, to signal election results. A northward beam signaled a majority for Republicans and a southward beam signaled a majority for Democrats.

The first Macy's Thanksgiving Day Parade in 1924 was called the "Macy's Christmas Day Parade" although it took place on Thanksgiving Day. It included camels, goats, elephants, and donkeys. The original route was from 145th Street and Convent Avenue to 34th Street and Herald Square.

The Macy's Thanksgiving Day Parade is now the world's second largest consumer of helium after the

U.S. government. Due to a helium shortage in 1958, the balloons were brought down Broadway on cranes.

In 1965, New York City began its ad campaign "Save water: shower with a friend" after five years of drought.

On October 29, 1945, more than 5,000 excited shoppers crammed into Gimbels Department Store on West 33rd Street in Manhattan to see the latest innovation: the ball-point pen.

On June 25, 1906 architect Stanford White was shot to death by the jealous husband (Harry Thaw) of his former lover, (Evelyn Nesbitt) atop his own creation, Madison Square Garden.

LULLABY OF BROADWAY

Words by Al Dubin

Come on along and listen to
the Lullaby of Broadway.
The hip hooray and ballyhoo,
the Lullaby of Broadway

The rumble of a subway train,
The rattle of the taxis,
The daffydils who entertain
at Angelo's and Maxie's.

When a Broadway baby says "Good night,"
It's early in the morning,
Manhattan babies don't sleep tight
until the dawn:

Goodnight, Baby,
Goodnight,

Milkman's on his way,
Sleep tight, Baby,
Sleep tight,
Let's call it a day,
Hey!

Come on along and listen to
the Lullaby of Broadway.
The hideehi and boopadoo,
the Lullaby of Broadway

The band begins to go to town,
And ev'ry one goes crazy,
You rockabye your baby 'round
'til ev'rything gets hazy.
"Hush-a-bye, I'll buy you this and that,"
You hear a daddy saying,
And baby goes home to her flat
to sleep all day:

Goodnight, Baby,
Goodnight, Milkman's on his way,
Sleep tight, Baby,
Sleep tight,
Let's call it a day.
Listen to the lullaby of old Broadway.

IN PRAISE OF NEW YORK

THOMAS M. DISCH

As we rise above it, row after row
Of lights reveal the incredible size
Of our loss. An ideal commonwealth
Would be no otherwise,
For we can no more legislate
Against the causes of unhappiness,
Such as death or impotence or times
When no one notices,
Than we can abolish the second law
Of thermodynamics, which states
That all energy, without exception, is wasted.
Still, under certain conditions
It is possible to move
To a slightly nicer
Neighborhood. Or if not,
Then at least there is usually someone
To talk to, or a library
That stays open till nine.
And any night you can see Times Square
Tremulous with its busloads
Of tourists who are seeing all of this
For the first and last time
Before they are flown
Back to the republic of Azerbaidzhan
On the shore of the Caspian,
Where for weeks they will dream of our faces
Drenched with an unbelievable light.

*I*t'll be a great place if they ever finish it.

—O. HENRY

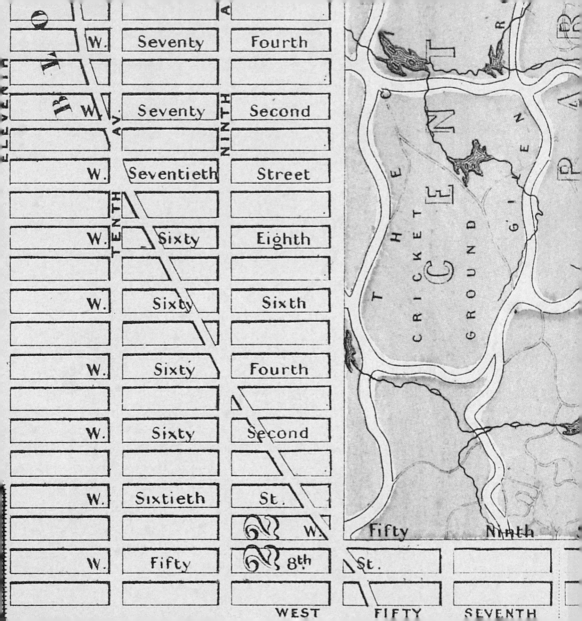